Newport laughed harshly

"Your little spy base is about to be blown off the face of the earth. While I'd like nothing more than to see that happen, I have problems of my own. Problems you are about to help me correct. That is, if you want to live and keep your little spy base. Your call. You've got about a minute and a half."

Bolan knew the bastard wasn't bluffing. "Where are they coming from?"

"Are you going to give me that Boy Scout helping hand?"

"What's the job?"

"I'll get in touch with you on the other side of this. Do I have your word, Lancelot?"

"Yeah. Where are they coming from?"

"South by southwest. Thirteen birds. You don't have a lot of time. I'll be in touch."

The line went dead.

MACK BOLAN ®

The Executioner

DON PENDLETON'S
THE EXECUTIONER®
ULTIMATE PRICE

A GOLD EAGLE BOOK FROM
WORLDWIDE.®

TORONTO • NEW YORK • LONDON
AMSTERDAM • PARIS • SYDNEY • HAMBURG
STOCKHOLM • ATHENS • TOKYO • MILAN
MADRID • WARSAW • BUDAPEST • AUCKLAND

To the legions of Bolan watchers the world over.
This one's for you.

First edition January 2001
ISBN 0-373-64266-0

Special thanks and acknowledgment to
Gerald Montgomery for his contribution to this work.

ULTIMATE PRICE

Guard, protect and cherish your Land for there is no afterlife for a place that started out as Heaven.

—Charles M. Russell
Montana, 1929

Every so often a great evil rises up to accost hearth and home. Always, we rise to the challenge and beat back the enemy. We must—to survive.

—Mack Bolan

THE
MACK BOLAN®
LEGEND

Nothing less than a war could have fashioned the destiny of the man called Mack Bolan. Bolan earned the Executioner title in the jungle hell of Vietnam.

But this soldier also wore another name—Sergeant Mercy. He was so tagged because of the compassion he showed to wounded comrades-in-arms and Vietnamese civilians.

Mack Bolan's second tour of duty ended prematurely when he was given emergency leave to return home and bury his family, victims of the Mob. Then he declared a one-man war against the Mafia.

He confronted the Families head-on from coast to coast, and soon a hope of victory began to appear. But Bolan had broken society's every rule. That same society started gunning for this elusive warrior—to no avail.

So Bolan was offered amnesty to work within the system against terrorism. This time, as an employee of Uncle Sam, Bolan became Colonel John Phoenix. With a command center at Stony Man Farm in Virginia, he and his new allies—Able Team and Phoenix Force—waged relentless war on a new adversary: the KGB.

But when his one true love, April Rose, died at the hands of the Soviet terror machine, Bolan severed all ties with Establishment authority.

Now, after a lengthy lone-wolf struggle and much soul-searching, the Executioner has agreed to enter an "arm's-length" alliance with his government once more, reserving the right to pursue personal missions in his Everlasting War.

Stony Man Farm, Virginia

Mack Bolan tried to ignore the ringing phone. Moments like this didn't grace his world very often and when the time was right, Mack Bolan put everything he had into the act. Hour by hour, he never knew if this might be his last one. He had to live every moment of his life as if it were his last hour, performing every act in every moment fully conscious that his old partner Death might be waiting for his number next. Bolan knew that when Death came for him, he'd go over the threshold with nothing left unsaid. No loose ends.

No goodbyes would be necessary.

She smelled like a woman untouched by modesty. Her perfume was sweat, musk and hot breath, and his inner animal responded accordingly. And had been most of the night. She didn't try to mask the smells God gave her. She practiced proper hygiene but beyond that she was an all-natural woman.

And Mack Bolan was an all-American man.

But that goddamn telephone was ruining everything.

Price was gasping beneath him, carving furrows into his back.

Bolan gave it up and rolled off her.

"The world always finds a damn crisis when I'm trying to show a girl a good time," he muttered.

"Yeah, I hear that, soldier."

Well, at least his ego wasn't going to suffer.

Bolan reached out and plucked the phone off the hook and put it to his ear. He was expecting to hear Hal Bologna's voice or Aaron Kurtzman's. He visibly tensed as the recognition sunk in. Price sensed the foreboding in her lover's posture and put a hand on his back.

"It's about time you picked up, friend," the voice said. "Two more minutes and this phone call would have been redundant."

It was Lance Finnig, aka Joe Newport. The fact that the bastard could call Bolan on his personal line at the Farm spoke volumes for the man's reach, his resources. Ever since Denver, Bolan had been keeping a quiet eye out for Deputy Director Lance Finnig of FEMA, and the guy seemed to have dropped off the face of the earth. Bolan was starting to think that the son of a bitch was on one of those helicopters that were blown out of the sky by Stinger missiles over Buckley.

Obviously, that wasn't the case.

"So you're not dead after all. Guess I'm going to have to try harder this time."

Newport laughed harshly.

"Oh, you screwed things up real good for me in Denver. So don't get all down on yourself. But I'm doing you a favor tonight, so you're going to owe me."

"I don't think so."

"Oh, I *know* so. How badly do you want to keep that little spy base of yours?"

Bolan cued in on that threat immediately.

"I'm listening."

"Your little spy base is about to be blown off the face of the earth. While I'd like nothing more than to see that happen, I have problems of my own. Problems *you* are going to help me correct. That is, if you want to live and keep your little spy base. You want to keep all that or not? Your call. You've got about a minute and a half."

Bolan knew that the man wasn't bluffing.

"Where are they coming from?"

"Are you going to give me that Boy Scout helping hand?"

"What's the job?"

"I'll get in touch with you on the other side of this. Do I have your word, Lancelot?"

"Yeah. Where are they coming from?"

"South by southwest. Thirteen birds. You don't have a lot of time. You better start getting your ass in gear. I'll be in touch."

The line went dead.

Bolan touched a button on the phone. It was a silent

alarm. He grabbed a pair of trousers off the bureau and put them on quickly.

"What's going on?" Price asked.

On his way out the door, Bolan said, "We're about to be attacked. You better get dressed."

And he ran for the elevator.

Camp Perry

WHEN THE MIGHTY FELL, it was a long way to the bottom. The impact was usually rude and unforgiving. Joe Newport had been a man to be feared. A man other men avoided annoying or disturbing in any way. Newport was the kind of guy mafiosi would issue a black ace to and turn loose on the competition.

That was in the days before Bolan.

But Newport had been double-timed and literally ground into the earth by this unbelievable bastard, left alive to suffer the indignities of his peers before being mercifully snuffed out for good. Newport had been thrown off COMCON—the Committee to Suspend the Constitution—relieved of his duties as SENSOPS chief of operations and stripped of the very uniform he institutionalized. In the wake of the spectacular burnout and backfire of his plans to bring down Bolan in Denver, Newport wasn't even his code name anymore. He was made aide de camp to the new SEN-SOPS chief and told to wear the plumage of his new place in the hierarchy of things: a brown suit, shirt, tie and leather Oxfords, polished to a mirror-perfect shine. The entire COMCON apparatus was to refer to the former chief only as Mr. Brown.

It was an ugly about-face.

Newport had been high and mighty for too long to allow this reversal to go unvindicated. On both sides.

The Bolan effect couldn't be defused. Newport's plans were shattered like expensive Hollywood stunt glass. At least he would live long enough to outlive his soon-to-be former peers on the Committee. Newport was going to clear the board and seize the mantle of destiny himself. The destiny of the Fourth Reich, the once and future architect of everything that should have been.

If not for one man.

That son of a bitch—that principled bastard.

Newport had to stop thinking about what could have been, what should have been had that son of a bitch Senator Mannix not brought this hellfire bastard into the loop. Mannix was running a tab with Joe Newport, as well. The Committee, Mannix, Bolan— they were all going to get what was coming to them. Newport would personally see to that.

But first things first.

The new SENSOPS chief, Tristan Zeigler, had to go.

Newport had no doubts that Bolan would be able to turn a two-minute warning into the rudest awakening Zeigler would ever experience. It was just too damn bad that he couldn't have arranged for a video feed from that jackal's chopper, so Newport could see what kind of expression would twist that greedy little bastard's face when he finally realized he'd been had.

Newport was a stay-behind. He knew it was all part of the snub, the loss of status, like wearing the brown suit. Brown being the color of shit. It was a bitter bucket of shit to have to swallow. Because the Committee sentenced him to *this,* living in the shadow of his former self as nothing more now than a gofer instead of killing him had sealed their fates.

They should have killed him.

He wasn't a man to humiliate. No, sir.

Newport had been left in the open-bay barracks that the Werwolf strike troops billeted in while preparing for this sneak attack. Zeigler told him to work on his shoes. When Zeigler returned, he wanted to be able to shave using Newport's brown Oxford shoes as a mirror.

Those shoes were dropped, unpolished, onto the wadded-up brown suit, and Newport soaked the pile with lighter fluid. He emptied the can and tossed it after the shoes. The offensive clothing was on the bunk he'd been assigned.

He removed the half-smoked pack of menthol cigarettes from the breast pocket of the black suit coat and tapped one out, putting the cigarette in his mouth. He replaced the cigarette pack while pulling the gold-plated lighter from his pants pocket—pants that were black, too. He glanced at his feet while lighting up and saw the flame and his face mirrored perfectly in the obsidian glow of immaculately spit-shined black Oxford shoes.

He took a deep drag off the smoke, clicking the lighter shut with a snap. He exhaled and took another puff.

"Goodbye, Mr. Brown," he said, and dropped the cigarette onto the heap.

He turned and walked calmly down the center aisle between the two rows of bunks as the flames danced merrily on his former bunk, reaching for the ceiling.

He exited into the night and didn't look back.

It was good to be himself again.

The War Room, Stony Man Farm

As MACK BOLAN FINISHED dressing, Aaron "the Bear" Kurtzman had patched into a surveillance satellite in geosynchronous orbit above the Eastern Seaboard and beamed it into the War Room. Bolan was suiting up for war. He had stepped into a pair of combat boots and stayed with the khaki cargo pants. Time for finding a shirt wasn't an option; he buckled a black assault vest over his bare torso.

Kurtzman was all over it. He knew very well what to look for from orbit—modest heat signatures flying in an aggressive formation.

The large screen on the wall came to life with a live feed from the covert orbiter.

While Kurtzman narrowed the search parameters looking for the incoming attack force, Bolan was barking orders over the tac net to Farm security personnel, led by Buck Greene.

"Buck, this is Striker. The Farm is about to be

attacked from the air. I need you to get your people oriented to the south-southwest. Get as many Stingers as you can carry and fire on anything you can lock on to. Put your men in outside the Ring of Fire. How copy?"

"Good copy. What's inbound?"

"You've seen Jack's new toy. About a baker's dozen just like it."

"ETA?"

"Any second."

Greene didn't bother to respond. Bolan knew that the man was springing into action, using these last precious moments to get the job done.

"Your intel is good, Mack," Kurtzman announced. "There they are."

Bolan looked at the screen and swore. The thirteen AeroDeth helicopters were flying in a diamond formation. The odd bird out was flying in the center of the diamond. That would be the Command and Control bird, Bolan thought.

"Activate ADA and see if Hal can get any fast movers on station from Patterson," the Executioner said.

He hefted the Barrett .50-caliber sniper system and ran for the elevator.

Kurtzman went to work.

Camp Perry

THE BARRACKS WERE visibly on fire and were drawing in the roving security teams like moths. Yelling, cursing and the sounds of frantic boot heels pounding on gravel augmented the crackle of the fire in the predawn stillness.

It was music to Joe Newport's ears.

He walked without a care in the world to the helipad where the reserve helicopter sat, the pilot standing by in the cockpit monitoring the emergency frequency. He stopped at the edge of the pad and lit up a cigarette. Two Werwolf troopers immediately converged on him.

"You aren't allowed here. Return to your place. Now."

The Werwolf emphasized his dire intent by clicking the select-fire switch on the silenced MP-5 off safe.

Newport wasn't impressed. He blew smoke at the biological automaton.

"My barracks is on fire."

"Your excuses are irrelevant."

No humanity lurked in either set of eyes. Their weapons were still at the ready, but Newport knew that would change immediately.

"When you're right, you're right," he said.

He threw down the cigarette while pulling the P-38 from inside his coat in the same motion. Newport hadn't lost the touch. The nasty little Walther banged twice and terminated any possible reaction from the sentries. The high-velocity 9 mm rounds caved in both foreheads and kicked the two soldiers backward off their feet.

Newport stepped over the twitching bodies and

boarded the AeroDeth. He squeezed through the narrow access into the cockpit and took the seat to the right of the pilot.

"Take us up, Mr. Kolchak," he said.

The pilot, Lon Kolchak, donned the flight helmet and fired up the engines.

"Yes, sir, Mr. Newport."

Newport had more surprises up his sleeve than a cheap magician. His associates on the Committee were stupid if they thought taking away his black suit and his command post would effectively neuter his ability to make things happen.

Now it was a matter of making sure that Bolan survived to see the dawn's early light and that weasel Zeigler didn't.

Stony Man Farm, Virginia

ON THE THIRD FLOOR of the main house, Mack Bolan turned at the sound of the elevator door opening.

His jaw dropped.

Barbara Price was dressed in a form-fitting combat blacksuit. Her feet were encased in black boots and crisscrossed over both shoulders were a dozen boxes of belted 7.62 mm NATO ammunition. A spare barrel bag was slung across her back. She hefted the latest cut-down version of the M-60 machine gun by the carrying handle in her right hand and a green Army-issue steel box of extra ammunition in her left hand. Her honey blond hair was pulled tight into a ponytail, and the grin on her face said she wasn't going to take no for an answer.

"I want to help," she said.

Bolan nodded.

"I know you're qualified."

"Damn right I am. Staying behind like I do, I get lots of range time in."

"You have a good nose for weapons systems."

She set down the ammo can and hefted the snubby M-60 in both hands.

"I love this gun," she said.

Bolan bit down on the urge to correct her. The M-60 was allowed the verbal reference of "gun." The M-60 was called the Big Gun and alternately, the Hog or the Pig. Had she decided to grab an M-16/ M-203 combo and call it all a "gun" would have been an infantry no-no. He had a split-second flashback to the image of irate drill instructors screaming at dumb recruits, "This is my weapon, this is my gun! This one's for killing and this one's for fun!" A military firearm, other than an M-60 or field artillery, was *never* referred to as a gun. Raw recruits discovered that fact the hard way, by doing push-ups until the drill instructor got tired watching. Drill instructors never came close to visual exhaustion until the offending recruit was smoked worse than a Jimmy Dean sausage.

Physical training could be a wonderful correctional tool.

The third floor of the main house was one large open area. The square footage was earmarked for storage and was designed to function as a defense level, as well. Shooters had 360-degree coverage of the grounds through one of the recessable bulletproof windows that were built liberally into the perimeter of the farmhouse. Mack Bolan had every window down. He was sure that he'd be running to all sides of the house soon enough, engaging targets of opportunity that were in the open.

The Executioner positioned Price in the window located in the southwest corner of the house, resting the M-60 on its bipod on the concrete parapet built for exactly this purpose. As a large number of the blacksuit security personnel were in the field with Able Team, he'd need all the fire support he could get.

Bolan pointed out her extreme left and right boundaries to the field of fire he was assigning her.

"Building 2 is your right boundary. The tractor barn is your left. Hose anything down inside that cone. When things get really insane down there, you'll have to lift and shift and run to whatever window seems to have the best killing opportunities. You'll be weapons free. Engage any targets at your discretion."

Price nodded soberly. She lifted the lid on the M-60 and fed belt number one into the king of the ambush. That done, she slammed the tray cover back in place and yanked back on the charging handle, locking the bolt carrier to the rear and compressing the firing spring. She flipped up the rear sight blade.

"Set your range for 300 meters," Bolan said.

Price clicked the sight blade up to the 300 mark.

Bolan heard a rustling in the night, like the approach of a swift but silent breeze.

They had arrived.

Kurtzman's voice crackled over the tac net, "Thirteen contacts just crossed into Stony Man airspace. Request for close air support has so far not been acknowledged. And backup air defenses are not yet online."

"Roger."

The Executioner hurried back along the south wall and took up his position covering the south-southwest with the sniper system. If he had the line of sight, the rifle could reach out and touch someone from a mile away, packing on the punch of speeding steel I-beam.

The enemy was about to strike Bolan on home turf. It was time to defend the hearth or die trying.

THE ATTACK FORMATION FLEW in over the southwestern fence line, five hundred yards north of the corner of the plot. From that approach, the slope of the land was rising. It took only seconds for the kill birds to clear the wooded terrain and enter the hilltop clearing that the main house and outbuildings occupied.

As soon as the helicopters cleared the tree line, the rocket pods began prepping the LZ on the main house. The whizzers launched in double-dozen clusters and found the mark. The trailing V in the diamond formation rose up, clearing the rotors of the birds flying in the forward V, and added six more sets of rocket pods into the blistering salvos.

The main house was engulfed in flame and fireballs. The structure was completely obscured by smoke, debris and fire. The attack went on hold to access damage. Shrubs and flowerbeds in the landscaping that ringed the main compound of Stony Man Farm "flipped over" and 20 mm Vulcan ADA turrets flopped up like trapdoor spiders, unleashing a curtain of explosive projectiles from the rotating barrels of the electric cannons. The diamond formation flew apart in all directions as the black helicopters peeled up, down, left and right to get out of those brutal cones of fire. The robot "eyes" on the turrets utilized infrared, radar and laser tracking systems to continuously orient and engage valid targets.

The cannons tracked the AeroDeth choppers as the evasive maneuvers were executed, maintaining an unbroken rate and volume of fire onto the targets.

On top of the hill, the fog of ordnance cleared enough to reveal the solid outline of the main house, still standing. The farmhouse was a Trojan horse; underneath what looked like a farmhouse was a frame of blast concrete reinforced with high-tensile steel and titanium. The facings fastened to the concrete bunker gave the structure a deceptively fragile cast. The farmhouse was all Hollywood special effect. The fortress beneath was hardcore. The farmhouse set decorations had been blown into sawdust and vinyl particles that hung in chunks and sticks off anchoring bolts in the concrete walls once hidden.

The structure hadn't been breached at all.

A booming muzzle-blast rolled across the open hilltop like summer thunder, a single titanic shot. The .50-caliber armor-piercing round breached the Command and Control helicopter. The small-arms resistant cockpit glass was punched through with a silver-dollar-sized hole, and the pilot's head liquefied inside the flight helmet. The aircraft was in the hands of a dead man and corkscrewed out of the sky and into the meadow.

Right on the heels of the thunderclap, a heavy machine gun opened up in choppy 6- to 9-round bursts.

From six different positions along the tree lines that ringed the hilltop, the chemical motors of Stinger missiles ignited and six javelins of death left launch tubes streaming into the deep purple skies.

The battle for Stony Man Farm had begun.

Georgetown, Maryland

GENERAL THURSTON WARD was a fit man for his age. He didn't have a paunch, and he ran almost every day for two miles. He was in a silk robe and boxers, sitting in his study alone after hanging up the phone following a conversation with the President. The Man had some commander-in-chief type orders for the Air Force to turn into operational reality.

And then there was the matter of the eyes-only memo that had materialized over the fax during the President's call. It was from the Air Force Office of Special Investigations headquartered at Bolling AFB

in Washington, D.C. OSI was the internal-affairs arm
of the Air Force. The organization technically had the
power to investigate anyone wearing Air Force blue,
including a general sitting on the Joint Chiefs of Staff
at the Pentagon.

It was a memorandum for record opening a case
file on one Thurston Ward for the early-morning
events of November 20. The loss of manpower and
equipment was under investigation with possible
criminal consequences.

The memo was written as if it had been composed
later in the day, after events he hadn't even ordered
yet were already said and done. The general hadn't
fallen off the cold war bus yesterday. Somebody was
giving him some good advice about the futility of
making that next phone call. The one he promised to
make on behalf of the President of the United States,
General Ward's boss.

He read the memo twice before folding it in two
and placing it on his desk.

He was looking across the room at the wall in front
of him. His eyes were on the plaque that framed his
oath of service as a United States Air Force Officer,
taken so long ago when an infinitely different and
younger man had graduated from the elite Air Force
Academy in Colorado Springs.

He hadn't thought about that oath or what it meant
in a long time. Too much exposure to Washington,
D.C., could do that to a man. Suck the loyalty and
honor right out of him.

He reflected back on this career, spanning more than forty years now.

It had been a good ride.

The general deposited the fax from OSI into the paper shredder next to his desk, then picked up the phone and made a phone call.

It just felt right.

Stony Man Farm, Virginia

THE SIX Stinger missiles played aggressive matchmakers with desperately reluctant dates. The Aero-Deth choppers were state-of-the-art and could probably stay in front of one of the heat-seeking javelins until the chemical engine burned up. The distance from launch point to target intersect was just too narrow to maneuver in *and* begin kicking in full power in a flat-out race against death.

The six birds were locked, and it was a lock that couldn't be picked.

The pilots didn't just lollygag in the sky. Each one dropped or jerked or accelerated in different extreme changes of direction and angular orientation before being blown out of the sky.

Bolan's sniping of the Command and Control helicopter made for seven. Not bad for an opening salvo.

A little advance warning was all it took to sometimes turn the tides of entire battlefields.

The Stony Man defenders weren't about to let their early lead slip.

The surviving AeroDeth helicopters scattered back

across the tree line, staying low while the pilots used targeting scans of the hilltop defense to program the second missile launch. It took about two heartbeats before the rocket pods in both "fists" of the hovering six aircraft spit flame and gray smoke. The missiles whizzed back into the perimeter, dropped and scattered, splitting up and concentrating on one of six Vulcan robot turrets defending the southwestern arc.

Those gun turrets were silenced in what amounted to cluster bombing with Sidewinders. The fireballs were stillborn as the six stealth choppers boomed back onto the hilltop, storming the line before ground teams in the trees could lock them up again with Stingers.

The black helicopters hovered thirty feet off the ground between the tractor barn and Building 2. The anchors dropped almost simultaneously, deploying the six fast ropes that were in use before the plates hit the ground. The black-clad storm troopers literally dropped out of the belly of the beasts, one after the other, using the rope as a guide to the ground.

From the third-floor corner of the main house-bunker, an M-60 machine gun opened fire with a menacing deep-throated roar, harvesting souls in the fields of fire below. The burst lasted less than three seconds and stopped as two of the attack helicopters answered with electric cannon fire.

From the window in the bump-out, the Barrett roared and another pilot's head exploded like tapioca blood pudding inside the cockpit, spinning earth and sky together as spastic hands let go of the joystick.

The weird scorpion-shaped helicopter keeled over in the sky and kissed the dirt. The bird went down rotors first, right on top of a deploying front of the Werwolf troopers.

About forty men were reduced to carved chunks of flesh in a 360-degree fantail of high-velocity splatter. The rotors tried to slice dirt and blew apart as the upside down fuselage crumpled into the middle of the slaughter floor, breaking to pieces as the chunks of rotor flew away from the crash in all directions at an average height of thigh level.

Twenty more enemy troops were scythed down like chaff with seriously disfiguring injuries that killed most of the soldiers outright. Survivors lay on their backs kicking leg stumps that jetted blood in spurts that mimicked the heartbeat. Their eyes were glassy with programmed shock responses that took over in a mortal crisis. Pain receptors were deadened with biofeedback and the heartbeat slowed, coagulation mechanisms kicked into overdrive by powerful directives from the psychotronically conditioned brain.

It was a textbook example of what one shot from one well-trained sniper could do to the development of a battlefield, one shot to turn the tide very quickly with heavy loss of life for the enemy. It was a tactically brilliant fire decision to take out that helicopter hovering above a large mass of enemy ground troops. The rotor fragments caused even more bloody destruction, and about half the attack force was taken out of the play.

2

Bolan anticipated that the nearest two choppers would pivot toward the winking globe of the M-60, the most obvious target, and answer with the nose cannons. He went down and yelled over the tac net, "Barbara! Get down!"

The M-60 stopped bellowing, and he heard the big gun clattering to the concrete floor in time to Price's body thump right alongside the scaled-down weapons system. The twin bull-alligator roars of the Vulcan cannons filled the air with menacing vibrations, and the 20 mm rounds exploded impotently against the thick concrete walls that stood stoutly underneath the facade.

Bolan popped back up in his window and quickly made the target selection. The .50-caliber weapon exploded with a huge muzzle-blast, and the recoil was like being slammed in the shoulder with an oar. The Executioner rode the recoil halfway up and fought it there, tearing the barrel back down on the bipod onto the parapet. He assessed his shot through the 20-power scope.

His target bird was upside down and making

mincemeat of the troopers under the rotors. The crash turned the main blades into whirling meat cleavers that killed and maimed twenty more. The Werwolf troops left alive came out of the prone position in a run, jumping over the fallen that writhed but cried out very little.

The Executioner lurched forward and hit the window control button. The bulletproof glass pane hissed back up over the open firing port as he hit the deck.

Perhaps three of the five remaining helicopters answered with rocket pods zeroed on Bolan's abandoned firing hole. The raised glass detonated the missiles that would have otherwise sailed into the interior and filled the space with a roasting flash fire. As an afterthought, Bolan raised the rest of the covers over the firing parapets at the first control panel he encountered along the south wall. He punched in a secondary command, and dense armor plates slid down over the inches-thick glass.

Short of a tactical nuke, the level was just about breach proof.

Over the tac net, Bolan heard the two telltale screeches of launching Stingers as Buck Greene yelled orders to his maneuver elements.

"I need coverage in the south! Stone Echo! Flank and pin down these ground troops! Everyone else concentrate on maintaining effective ADA!"

Bolan stayed low as he jogged the rest of the way to Price. He was enough of a battlefield pragmatist to know nothing was foolproof.

The gutsy woman was squatting over her weapon.

The feed-tray cover was up, and she was throwing off a 5-round scrap while pulling a fresh belt out of a box. She laid the links in place and slammed down the lid. The bolt was already locked to the rear.

She stood and put her hands on her hips.

"Well? Now what?"

The farmhouse shook violently as another dozen rockets detonated across the southern face of the building, and the vibrations were heavy enough to throw Price off balance. Bolan maintained his center and leaned forward, reaching out to steady the woman. She wrapped fingers around Bolan's forearm and regained her center. The shaking passed quickly. Dust fell from the ceiling and the lights flickered.

"Those pesky termites," Price said.

"We're going to need one hell of a big can of Raid."

STINGERS TOOK DOWN one more chopper and shook up the second enough to give the pilot something to think about. The damaged helicopter fell to the rear and let the three full-strength AeroDeths face the opposition first. The four black helicopters hovered on the upslope of the southern spread, just beyond the tractor barn and Building 2. The point aircraft stayed oriented on the main house. The flanking choppers pivoted in midair ninety degrees to the left and right of the point aircraft, covering the avenues of approach from the east and west. The damaged bird spun and covered the south.

The tactics and maneuver formations of attack helicopters weren't much different from those used by ground infantry. The concept was the same: move fast, move quietly and move with the best all around security. The same tactics essentially remolded and applied to things that moved around and fought in the sky.

It was the damaged aircraft that made the first kill.

The AI assistant running alongside the onboard targeting software "saw" the Army-issue Hummer creeping up through the trees, moving to engage the ground troops maneuvering in the open toward the main house. The targeting options came to life in the pilot's visor, and he made the decision to open fire with rockets.

Four missiles off the left pod flew in a corkscrew pattern into the target. Two of the missiles detonated in the dirt right in front of the Hummer, and the other two took the military ATV broadside. The vehicle went to hell in the fireballs, coming apart while being flipped like a flapjack, wheels over roof and back down to earth again.

There were no survivors.

Three more Stinger missiles launched from three different locations along the east-south-west arc of the hilltop, from inside the trees but close enough to the open to maintain good line of sight. All three of the man-packed missiles triangulated on the damaged chopper, vengeance delivered while comrades' souls were still dissipating with the smoke on the predawn breeze.

The missiles made short work of the gunship, smearing it out of existence like a bad finger painting.

The flanking birds pivoted as soon as the missiles made that shotgun boom and shot out the disposable launch tubes locked and loaded. The targeting sensors on both black gunships had the Stinger positions counterlocked and took turns hitting all three positions with a mix of rockets and nose cannons.

Those three patches of real estate burned out of control like fiery slashes in the landscape. No more missiles would be fired from those locations. The attack birds rocked back and forth across the rear arc of the killing fields, looking for other pockets of resistance to reveal their locations with muzzle-flashes, rocket launches or body-heat signatures.

A pause in the fighting fell over the battlefield.

It was short-lived.

BUCK GREENE LOWERED the night-vision binoculars and cursed.

Security teams Stone Echo and Stone Bravo were gone. Charlie was in the north, waiting for orders. Greene was Stone Alpha leader. His fire team was still one hundred percent. They had a camo-painted Hummer parked behind the berm, which concealed beneath it the blast-proof concrete vault that housed one of the numerous MCPs—Munitions Cache Points—scattered all over the Farm. Each MCP was fully stocked to cover every conceivable threat scenario Bolan and his experts could dream up in their worst nightmares of being surrounded and overrun.

Stony Man Farm could hold out for quite some time in an extended confrontation. As long as there were still soldiers left to expend ammo, there was a hell of a lot of boom socked away for that rainy day all over the plot. All four buildings clustered on the open hilltop were armed to the teeth, as well; every floor had a weapons room or armory of some kind. Ready access to firearms would never be a problem in a crisis.

Greene lay on his belly like a lizard, just enough of him peeking up over the top of the berm to use the NVD binoculars.

He was looking for movement, evidence of survivors of any kind. There was no more radio traffic from Echo or Bravo. It didn't bode well for those men. The main house was still under siege, and the remaining enemy ground troops were holding the hilltop almost unopposed.

That had to change.

He backed off the top of the berm, staying on his belly, crabbing to the rear about five feet. A mottled mound of earth moved and came to life next to him. It was his second-in-command. The two leaned into each other, and Greene whispered directly into the other man's ear.

"I want all the ammo and extra missile rounds each of us can carry put into rucksacks. We're going to contour around the hill to the north, link up with Charlie and go up the hill from the opposite side. We're moving out in less than ninety seconds. Make it happen."

The other man slithered with very little noise to the bottom and went into the cache vault to make things happen.

THE MAIN HOUSE was ringed with Claymore mines on all sides thirty yards out and twenty yards apart. The mines were armed remotely and triggered from security consoles inside the house, since the Annex wasn't yet fully functional. None of the mines were booby trapped. A human being at a computer console had to be monitoring the mines, activate and manually fire the antipersonnel devices. There could be no accidents among friendlies that way.

The southwestern corner was fired from the security office, six mines in all. The charging Werwolf commandos, almost sixty of them left, were crossing the last line of defense. The detonation shredded the first ones in, about ten of the troops, and took down fifteen more that were within the effective kill zone for the mines. The survivors were left with a cleared front, and the black-clad soldiers of the Fourth Reich made it to the main house.

Cosmetically, most of the rear of the farmhouse was blown into slivers of mortar, wood and vinyl siding, set dressing that had been anchored to the bombproof concrete box underneath. A porch had stretched along the entire southern face of the house, from the bump out to the western corner: white wood deck, rails and columns.

The porch was completely blasted to rubble. The exposed concrete was pocked and smoke blackened.

The bank of windows along the southern exposure was false. Just real double-pane windows and enough space between the glass and the concrete to hang a set of folksy-looking curtains in. All that was gone now. Fires burned in patches all over the back lawn of the main house, and the enemy troops jigged around the obstacles.

From inside the security office, the closed-circuit television monitors covered the charge on the house.

"We got incoming!" Brad Paddock announced from the security control suite.

Rich Solon, on station with Paddock, was in the small armory built off the security office, stacking magazines and weapons on the counter for a panic issue. He didn't feel good about his comrade's exclamation. Something ugly was about to happen; he could feel it in his bones.

The foundation of the house shook again with a munitions-based earthquake.

Out in the office, Paddock was in communication with the surviving members of that morning's security detail.

"Roger, they've made the southern face of the main house," Paddock reported. "They're up to something back there. Deploying something out of rucks."

There was a squelch of static, then Greene's voice.

"Keep us updated. We're downslope on the north side, moving up toward the house now."

On the monitors, the ominous black-clad Werwolf killers worked like harmonious ants. In groups of five, the troops were uncoiling what looked like a hose or rope and affixing it to the concrete wall and the steel coded access door in big, man-size ovals. There were seven big ovals in all. Spaced about every two feet along the length of each thick cord was what looked like a gel pack of some kind. Whatever these people were deploying, it was obviously going to be used as some kind of cutting charge to breach the walls and door.

Paddock knew something about the construction of the buildings on Stony Man Farm. The concrete in the walls was two feet thick, with steel reinforcements latticed throughout the aggregate. It would take one hell of a boom to breach that. Paddock couldn't imagine that those coils packed that much firepower locked inside in some esoteric chemical stasis. Based on Striker's past briefings on this enemy, Paddock knew that these zealots were higher up on the scales of scientific achievement than the NSA and were fielding equipment that belonged fifty years in the future.

Paddock's sense of dread multiplied as he watched the perfectly efficient moves each trooper went through to complete the mission.

When the work was done, the troops backed away and lowered the dark goggles on the front of the Nazi-style battle helmets over their eyes. The goggles reminded Paddock of the serious eye protection that arc welders used to keep their eyes from frying in the glare.

He had that sinking feeling in his stomach, like an elevator in free fall.

"Oh, shit," he breathed.

Whatever those coils were, ignited.

It was like the surface of the sun brought down to earth. Much brighter than white phosphorous. The savage level of photon emissions was more than the closed-circuit TV camera could endure. The monitors bleached out, then lost the picture altogether.

The security-office door opened into the dining room. Straight across the formal dining room was the coded access door that opened onto the back porch. Hellish incandescent light seared the south wall, light so powerful and hot that it shone through two feet of concrete like waxed paper. That light became even more intense, and the temperature in there was instantly above a hundred degrees.

Then the plugs were pulled on the demon light as seven synchronous explosions pulped the superheated concrete and steel, blowing concrete coals and semi-molten metal across the beautifully decorated formal dining room, instantly setting off hundreds of little fires from floor to ceiling all over the room.

A superheated blast of debris blew into the security office through the open doorway. Paddock's back was to the door, and his chair, shoulders, head, the console and wall in front of him caught fire like raw gasoline.

In the small armory, Solon almost lost the contents of his bladder as the adjoining office went up in flames and the screams of his buddy cut like bloody fingernails across the frontal lobes. Solon went into action. He grabbed the small fire extinguisher from under the counter and bounded into the burning office, shielding his face with his forearm as he sprayed the white foam on Paddock. The man was burning from the shoulder blades up while screaming and careening from wall to wall, trying to smash out the flames.

Paddock sank to the floor moaning. The guy was burned very badly.

Solon took a step toward his fallen comrade, but the sounds of dozens of boot heels grinding debris underfoot spun him toward the open door.

He didn't have time to draw his .357 Desert Eagle before being zipped from sternum to Adam's apple by dozens of 9 mm rounds. He was dead before he hit the floor.

The security office was shut down permanently.

And the main house was breached.

Second Floor, Main House

MACK BOLAN CAME OFF the last step and went low, peering around the corner to his left, looking down the short corridor. The air was choked with smoke and dust; the grounds were off the grid now. Emergency lights were making ominous apparitions out of the shape-shifting fog. But the corridor was empty. For now. Bolan inched farther around the corner and grabbed a surreptitious look down the stairs to the first floor. The alcove and entryway were choked with smoke, and reflected firelight glistened on the white textured walls like shadow play.

He heard the shouts in German down there and

knew things were about to get very busy. Bolan had no doubts that these bastards had a very good idea already of how the house was laid out. The basement would be a high-priority target to them. They'd be sending a force upstairs, as well. That was just good tactics.

The Executioner tucked back into the stair alcove to the third floor. Price was crouched at the ready halfway to the landing, waiting for Bolan's word.

"Two seems clear for now," Bolan said. "We've got party crashers downstairs. You're going to cover the stairs while I get something better suited for room-to-room fighting."

Price nodded soberly.

The Executioner guided Price to her firing position. He placed her in the prone with the chopped-off M-60 resting on its bipod on the first step down, covering the landing without having to take aim. Just squeeze and hose. Bolan knew that nobody was going to get by her without paying the ultimate price.

Bolan kissed her on the forehead and took off into the smoke to eat the enemy while they tried to digest him whole. Bolan was going to give them all a fatal case of stomach flu.

He knew that once the enemy realized the stairs were a deathtrap, the elevator would be the only other way up. Bolan hooked into the main corridor that ran the length of the main house. The elevator was located on the east end of the floor, opening to face the east wall. He plucked a fragmentation grenade off his assault vest and pulled the pin. He kept the spoon compressed in his fist and crouched in front of the elevator door. Bolan put the grenade on the carpet and butted it right into the V where the door slid into the frame. The weight of the grenade rested on top of the spoon, keeping it from flying and starting the cook off to detonation.

The soldier looked around him. A piece of drywall shaped like a shark's tooth was the most eligible piece of debris available. The Executioner used the fragment to act as a makeshift brace to hold the expedient booby trap in place until somebody came up the elevator and tried to get off on the second floor.

That done, Bolan retraced his steps and proceeded to his quarters on the second floor, located in the southeastern corner.

The bedroom had seen better days.

The southern face of the main house had weathered a hellish onslaught of firepower since 4:00 a.m. The two bulletproof windows in Bolan's suite, both on the south wall, hadn't stood up to the heavy shelling. They were jagged holes that only resembled the shape of a rectangle. The room was choked with smoke from the burning bed and sections of carpet closest to the south wall. The chest of drawers and bureau were ruined in the concussions of incoming ordnance, shattered into kindling and charred items of clothing.

Bolan wasn't here for extra socks.

There was a mirrored set of sliding glass doors against the west wall with a numerical keypad built into the drywall left of the frame. The mirrored glass was blasted into silica sand splattered on the carpet, revealing the battle steel beneath.

Bolan stayed in the hallway, soaking up every detail of the wrecked suite, looking for the danger that he felt like a physical companion.

His eyes narrowed. Framed in the jagged opening of one of the bedroom's windows was one of the black helicopters, hovering, nose gun and rocket pods locked on to the main house, scanning for any signs of resistance.

Bolan froze. He melted into the door frame and went low.

A lot of the bedroom was burning, and the heat of those fires obviously masked his own IR signature in the death bird's sensors.

Slowly, he raised the .50-caliber sniper rifle and adjusted the scope for the close-range conditions. The silhouette of the pilot swam into resolution through the 20-power sniper scope. Bolan put the crosshairs at center mass and squeezed the trigger like a lover's caress.

The noise of the muzzle-blast traveled for miles in the sound-conductive atmosphere of the predawn morning. The pilot never heard the shot that killed him. He saw the flash on infrared, then his life winked out.

Bolan called it a target of opportunity and he took it.

Another one bit the dust.

The death bird dropped from view and crashed to the turf below. Bolan was clear and he darted into the suite. He flattened against the wall next to the sliding doors and punched his code into the keypad.

The steel doors parted in the middle, recessing into the walls. Behind the doors was a closet devoted to the devices of death dealing. Bolan didn't have to fumble for what he wanted. He knew what to grab from the get-go.

He cached the sniper rifle in the closet and plucked the SWA-12 assault shotgun off the wall. He slammed a magazine of deer slugs into the weapon and yanked back the charging handle. He filled empty pouches on his vest with spares for the shotgun, placing only the same ammunition types into each ammo pouch. He took buckshot, slugs and HE with him.

The discharge of the .50-caliber rifle had attracted attention from downstairs. A group attempted to investigate only to be pinned down and shredded in the bellow of Price's M-60 machine gun.

Bolan grabbed an extra box of fragmentation grenades, jogged back to Price's position and set the box on the floor. He jerked a fragger off his vest, yanked out the pin and tossed the deadly egg down the stairwell. The spoon shot off and the fat little bomb rolled around the landing and down into the entryway before going off.

The explosion was quick and sharp; the screams of the dying were frosting on the cake.

Suppressed weapons fired into the entryway in impotent response. Bolan tossed another bomb down there for good measure and attacked the extra box of munitions, pulling grenades from cardboard cylinders and hanging them on his vest. He rationed out four of the HE eggs to Barbara.

''Use them wisely,'' he said, and shotgun at the ready, went down the stairs.

The North Face of the Main House

THE TWO TROOPERS dropped to one knee at the tree line and made the hand-and-arm signal for all clear. Greene ran forward, the rest of Alpha team with Charlie trailing in reserve. Greene scanned the area with night-vision goggles and satisfied himself that an ambush wasn't lying in wait.

He told his second-in-command to take the strike force onto the front porch and spread out, holding in place. His second nodded and sent the word back down the line. Under cover of right and left security, the assault force crossed the open area one man at a time and lined up against the north face of the main building, under the roof awning overhanging the front porch.

Greene went across as the last man before right and left security packed it up and joined the main assault force on the front porch. He went to the front door and considered the touch pad on the frame above the bell.

Pete Kendricks, Greene's number two, stood on the other side of the door, his back to the wall, and whispered, ''What's the plan? Pop the lid and go in?''

Greene held up his index finger.

Wait one.

"Striker, this is Buck," Greene said over the radio. "What's your twenty? You still in the main house, over?"

From the other side of the front door came three terrific thunderclaps so close together only an expert ear could separate the reports. Greene's ear was that good. He recognized the booms. It was that new assault shotgun that Striker had taken a liking to recently.

Greene got his answer.

ON THE OTHER SIDE of the coded access door, Mack Bolan came off the stairs firing. The entryway was littered with debris from the grenade blast, and three of the Werwolf troopers were pulling fallen comrades out of the area by the collar. Bolan turned the rescue team into casualties, too. Three explosive reports from the SWA-12 slapped those troopers stone cold dead, all of them jerked backward on invisible strings into the dining-room fire pit.

Buck Greene was trying to raise Bolan on the tac net, but the Executioner didn't have time for small talk.

Shouts of alarm came from back there, and Bolan tossed a grenade around the corner, into the dining room. He didn't wait for it to go off, but he bounded across the tiled entryway and crashed through the flimsy remains of the double French doors into the den. Two more Werwolf troopers were fighting to get through the doorway to Bolan's immediate left at the same time. The Executioner triggered a second trio of rounds from the combat shotgun and cleared the log-jam in the door.

The grenade went off in the dining room like doom. Bolan dropped the empty clip and fed a 9-round magazine of buckshot into the well. He slapped the bolt release and switched to single-shot mode.

The Executioner bolted to the left and took up a firing position in the doorway just cleared.

The fire-control systems came on-line at that time, and overhead nozzles fanned cool water into every room where sensors detected heat and smoke. It was a timely distraction.

From his angle on the action, Bolan had a perfect view of the dining room.

The place was a wreck. The long oak table in the middle of the room was gone, blown into toothpicks. The modest crystal chandelier that had been hanging over the table was just frayed wiring dangling from the blast-stripped ceiling. The coded access door was a slag-wreathed oval, and two more breach points were burned through the concrete walls on both sides. The water showering from the ceiling was turning the destruction into a sizzling bog of steam and standing pools.

The enemy was divided between the kitchen and the wreckage of the back porch. The dining room was littered with casualties from Bolan's grenade. Winking muzzle-flashes were erupting from the kitchen doorway and all three breach points, probing for Bolan's position.

The soldier stayed low and didn't offer them a target. Before he could respond, the M-60 machine gun hammered out a dialogue of death from the entryway, pinning down the shooters lurking on the other side of the breach points. Bolan saw movement flash from the kitchen doorway, and he shouldered the shotgun. A grenade flew across the battleground like a fastball off the pitcher's mound. The SWA-12 roared and Bolan's instincts were true.

It was like shooting skeet.

The wall of buckshot met the grenade halfway and deflected the bomb. That grenade was returned to sender and exploded in the doorway. Bolan shifted and triggered two more rounds toward the holes in the south wall.

There was a muffled boom from above and the ceiling shook.

Somebody had used the elevator access in the garage to try to attack from behind via the second floor. Bolan's booby trap had put an abrupt crimp in that plan.

The tide of the battle was turning in favor of the defenders.

The Executioner was blitzing.

"I SAY AGAIN!" Greene radioed. "This is Alpha team, and we're at the front door! We're coming in! Do not fire us up!"

He nodded to Kendricks.

"Open it."

Kendricks quickly punched in the five-digit code. The magnetic solenoids released with a metallic click, and the door was free. From the right side of the frame, Greene put a boot heel into the steel-core door and it swung open onto a fierce firefight. He went low and peered through the open doorway. He saw Price chest down on the tile behind the M-60 machine gun, firing precise bursts into the dining room. He didn't see Bolan anywhere.

He was taking a breath to shout out the order to enter the house when the dime was dropped.

One of the silent black helicopters had crossed over the house from back to front on a hunch. The pilot swung the bird around and dropped while cutting loose with the Vulcan cannon. The left flank of his assault force from the garage to midway down the length of the porch ceased to exist in fire and shrapnel. Kendricks and three others, all that remained of the left flank, were flung like rag dolls off the porch and into the grass. The men rolled and didn't get up. Greene was tossed through the open doorway and sent sprawling onto the tile floor. His head smacked into the bottom of the stairs.

Before the chopper could finish off the rest of Greene's security force, divine intervention stepped in to shore up those killer odds. Air-to-air missiles flew out of the darkness from the northeast and blew the enemy bird into oblivion. A second later, the scream of jet engines shook the hilltop as two F-16 fighters roared overhead at treetop level and banked straight up into the purple sky, twisting into a barrel roll to come around for a second pass.

The last of the whisper-quiet gunships broke off

and tried to run, and made it as far as the national forests bordering Stony Man Farm before being blown out of the sky.

The F-16 fighters made two more passes over the covert hardsite looking for any other aerial targets, then banked toward the ocean for the return flight back to the carrier USS *Enterprise*.

THE EXECUTIONER YANKED the pin and let the bomb fly. The grenade sailed across the dining room and outside. It exploded seconds later, clearing the breach points in.

"I'm coming across your front, Barb!" Bolan yelled. "Hold your fire!"

"Standing by!" she replied.

Bolan bounded out of the den and through the wreckage of the dining room. He dived through the kitchen doorway and rolled. As soon as he had crossed Price's field of fire, the M-60 was chopping away again, saturating the three breach points with covering fire.

The soldier came out of the shoulder roll onto his feet and scanned the room for viable targets. The grenade blast had devastated the cabinetry and the island in the center of the room. The skillets and pans that had been hanging over the island were lying twisted and peppered with holes all over the linoleum floor. The air was ripe with conflicting smells. The contents of the demolished spice rack fought for dominance over the odors of cordite, blood and seared flesh.

Bolan spotted movement to his front, from inside

the garage. Shadowy figures went low, and orange globes of fire blinked like strobes. The Executioner dived to the floor as subsonic 9 mm hornets chewed the woodwork, sounding like hatchet strikes.

He pulled another grenade off his vest and hooked his thumb through the ring.

He never got the pin out.

The soldier was vaguely aware of a serpentine hissing coming from the overhead ventilation but couldn't get his mind wrapped around that before the lights went out in his head and his world capsized into blackness.

The Main Gate

THE AERODETH HELICOPTER idled on the ground, ready to leap back into the sky at the first sign of danger, while Joe Newport stood in front of the stout-looking gates that opened onto Stony Man Farm. He taped a pink envelope at eye level right in the center.

Newport was giddy with good humor and couldn't keep from chuckling.

Inside the envelope was a get-well card to Mack Bolan along with a computer disk providing everything necessary for the role the big man would play in phase two of Newport's "readjustment" to the COMCON chain of command.

The overflight of the battleground had proved what Newport knew would be the outcome. The assault force had been completely neutralized. The hilltop was shrouded in drifting smoke, and fires burned in scattered patches inside and out of the tree line. The bodies of fighters on both sides of the conflict littered the hellgrounds like trash.

"From the fatherland, with love, you son of a bitch," Newport said.

Then he got out of there.

3

Mack Bolan awoke with a major headache.

He groaned and rolled onto his side, blinking away the fog that clouded his sight. It was light out now. His surroundings swam slowly back into focus.

Bolan was in the open-bay barracks occupying the second level of Outbuilding 1, in the bunk closest to the stairwell. He sat up and looked around. The other survivors, still out cold from the gas countermeasures, occupied the line of bunks on the latrine side of the floor. Price was in the bunk next to him. He counted ten of the blacksuits, and Buck Greene was the last in the line. The bunks against the opposite wall were all empty.

That couldn't be everybody who was left, he thought.

The churning in his guts told him otherwise.

Bolan swung his feet onto the cool concrete floor, the movement making his head spin. He took several steadying breaths before trying to get up. When he stood, he felt as if he were in danger of toppling over. That gas was serious stuff.

The ringing in his ears was pierced by the sound

of helicopters. Bolan staggered over to the big picture window in the middle of the bay on the opposite wall. The morning sun was high in the sky and painfully bright. From the angle of the light, he knew the time was between ten and noon. Was it still the same day or the next? He'd either been out for over five hours or close to thirty.

A CH-47 Chinook was landing on the lawn in the center of the four buildings on the hilltop. Federal troops were everywhere, as were the body bags—dozens and dozens of them. A platoon was on that detail. As soon as the loadmaster was clear of the ramp, soldiers began to haul the body bags inside the helicopter. Squads of soldiers were moving into and out of the tree line, scouring the slopes and woods for more survivors or more bodies. The wreckage of the enemy helicopters was cordoned off, surrounded by hazmat vehicles.

Directly below, Bolan spotted Hal Brognola in a suit that looked as if it had been slept in. The big Fed was gesturing with cigar in hand as he handed out orders to the Farm personnel.

The head Fed looked grim. But when he caught sight of Bolan in the window, his features relaxed and he waved.

Shoe leather pounded the stairs as Bolan headed in that direction on still wobbly knees. Brognola burst onto the second floor, his relief to find his friend well clearly evident.

"Striker! It's good to see you on your feet again! How are you feeling, guy?"

"Like hell," Bolan growled. He nodded at the bunks bedding down the rest of the Stony Man crew. "Is this all that's left, Hal?"

Brognola's face clouded over. "Yeah. A lot of the blacksuits didn't make it."

"Goddammit."

Vengeful anger was starting to burn through the narcotic fog of the knockout gas.

Finally, Bolan asked, "How bad's the damage?"

"Well, this is the worst beating the Farm's ever taken, but the collateral damage is mostly cosmetic. It'll take lots of elbow grease and rerouting some black budget funds to fix. But the men we lost today, hell, they're gone forever."

"But not in vain. I'll see to that."

Brognola nodded. "I'm going to bring Phoenix and Able back from the field."

Bolan shook his head. "No, don't do that. This is personal. I'll handle this alone."

"I think you should let me recall the men."

"Recall Jack. I'll need a pilot."

Brognola opened his mouth to argue the point but gave it up with a sigh. When Bolan made up his mind about something, that was it. All the demons in hell couldn't make this man turn away from a decision once it was made.

"I'll recall Jack, then. A contingent of blacksuits is already en-route."

"Has he made contact again?"

"Who? Jack?"

"No. Finnig. Newport. Whatever his damn name is. He said he'd be in touch again."

Brognola reached inside his suit coat, pulled out the pink envelope and handed it to Bolan.

"That was taped to the front gate when I arrived on the scene just before sunrise."

Bolan looked at the envelope front and back. The front of the envelope had an abrasion in the center of the paper, as though something adhesive had been torn away.

"What was on the front of the envelope, Hal?"

"Oh."

He reached into his trouser pocket and pulled out a red ribbon bow.

"This was."

"Cute."

"I thought so, too."

Bolan removed the card from the envelope. On the card was a picture of a busty blonde in a nurse's uniform. The caption read, "Hope you're not feelin' blue..." Bolan opened the card. "Get well soon." Under that was the message.

The only reason you're not dead yet is because you're worth more to me alive right now. The disk is your ticket to ride. You're invited to a dead man's party. Don't be late. I'm counting on you to react like the principled bastard you are.

Joe Newport

Bolan shook the disk out of the envelope. It was an Iomega 100-MB for a Zip drive.

"I've already had a look at it," Brognola stated.

"And?"

"It's everything you need to walk among them undetected. An identification template for a SENSOPS troubleshooter and an authentication matrix to encode on the magnetic strip of the ID card made from that template. You'll be bona fide FEMA."

"What about this party? When? Where?"

"Tomorrow in west Texas, just north of Midland. There are maps and blueprints of the complex in the target package. I get the distinct impression that Newport is in some sort of pissing contest with his elders and he wants you to help him eliminate the competition."

"Yeah, and then he's going to try to eliminate me."

"*Try* being the key word."

"Yeah."

"You know, Striker, with all the evidence we've got here in the wake of this attack, I can prosecute this by the book. I'm already assembling a task force. We've got prisoners this time. Seventeen of their shock troops. It might be good for the country my way. Reinstall a sense that our government still is accountable."

Bolan thought about that. He thought about the fact that the brain cells of this conspiracy had ordered the attack that had almost shut down Stony Man Farm forever. He thought about the fact that those faceless traitors would be waiting for news of the attack's outcome. Nobody in that assault was going to be reporting back to headquarters anytime soon.

"No, what we need now is a little disinformation. I see that a chopper full of newshounds was rounded up and forced down on the back lawn. What are your plans for them?"

"Charge them under federal law with trespassing and an aviation violation. This is restricted airspace. They saw things they should have never seen, and I think they're all going to do some time."

"I think you should cut them a deal they can't refuse. Edit their footage a little. Let them air the destruction and the body bags. Give them a cover story for them to air. A horrible training accident in the mountains with all hands lost. That's the key point I want going out over the airwaves—that everybody died. There were no survivors. Let's get that on national news so the right ears will hear the message we want them to hear."

"Then you go to Texas and crash their little summit."

"And they don't see me coming because they think I'm dead. Pay a visit to Senator Mannix while you're at it. They watch him very closely. Tell him point-blank that I died in this attack. Between the networks and the congressional grapevine, they'll get the word and they'll get the wrong impression."

Brognola frowned.

"It's comforting to know that devious mind of yours works for truth, justice and the American way. You'd really be dangerous if you were a criminal."

JIMMY PAYSON, reporter for WNNX in Arlington, was escorted into the operations tent with an armed guard on his right and left and a third covering the newsman from behind. The tent had been cleared of all personnel. The long fold-out table was cleared of sensitive documents and reports, the corkboard had been cleared of maps and the radios had been squelched, the frequency-dial readouts covered with tape so the reporter wouldn't be privy to the frequencies that the Feds were using.

Hal Brognola sat at the table, waiting. He pointed to a chair directly opposite him. "Please, have a seat, Mr. Payson."

Payson warily took a seat. Brognola nodded at the guards.

"That's all, men. I've got it."

The guards did an about face and exited the tent, leaving the two men alone at the bargaining table.

"Mr. Payson, I'm not going to throw the book at you, provided you do exactly what I say."

"Say nothing to no one, is that it? Or face federal charges?"

"Not quite."

Brognola placed a videotape on the table. He slid it across to Payson.

"I've edited the footage a little, but what's left is what you can air."

"You're going to let me air this story?"

"I'm going to let you air *a* story. This one."

A piece of paper appeared on the table next and

was slid across to Payson. The reporter picked up the paper and read it.

"This was a training accident, huh?"

"That's what it says."

"Special ops gone bad, huh?"

"That's what it says."

"Why're the hazmat suits here if this was just a training accident?"

"Standard environmental procedure with big fuel spills."

"Fuel spills?"

"Thirteen helicopters crashed here this morning. A serious amount of fuel went into the ground here. It needs a proper cleanup. EPA regs."

Payson looked at Brognola but didn't say anything. The big Fed could tell the newsman wasn't buying it at all, but the guy had no choice. He either played ball or he went to prison.

"Do we have a deal, Mr. Payson?" Brognola asked.

"What do I have to sign?"

Brognola smiled. "You and your crew will have to sign security disclosure agreements. These are very serious documents. Do not sign them and violate them, because I'll be there to prosecute all of you back into the Stone Age. Stick to the details of this incident exactly as I've given them to you. If you and your men can do all that, you're free to go within the hour."

Payson looked at the perfectly formatted and written news bite again.

"Okay. You've got a deal."

The Office of Senator John Mannix,
Capitol Hill, Washington, D.C.

WILMA THORNLEY, Senator John Mannix's secretary, buzzed him on the intercom and told him Hal Brognola was there to see him. The senator had the Justice man shown into his office immediately. Once the door was closed and she was back at her desk, Thornley pressed a red button on the phone console. An electrical current was sent into the senator's phone console, and the microphone in the mouthpiece was activated surreptitiously, allowing the secretary to hear everything that was being said in the office.

She listened intently to the conversation.

With a pad and paper, she transcribed the conversation in shorthand.

Mannix: It's good to see you, Mr. Brognola. What brings you here today?

Brognola: Perhaps you've seen the news about the Army training accident in Virginia this morning.

Mannix: Yes, I did.

Brognola: It was no accident.

Mannix: I see.

Brognola: Mack Bolan is dead, Senator. The incident in Virginia was a raid to take him out. All combatants on both sides died in the conflict. There were no survivors.

Mannix: Oh, my God. Those fascist bastards got him? I can't believe it.

Brognola: The Justice Department is going to pursue this all the way. We have enough evidence now to prosecute, and the President is behind me on this 110 percent.

Mannix: I'm in. I'm in. Just tell me what you need.

Brognola: I'm glad to hear that, Senator. You've got your finger on that pulse. I'll need your help.

Mannix: You've got it. Is there going to be a service for Bolan?

Brognola: No. His request was to be cremated and have the ashes scattered over his hometown in the event he ever died in combat. I'm going to honor that wish.

Mannix: This is a black day for this country. Nobody can replace that boy.

Brognola: You've got that right, sir. Striker liked you a lot. I thought you should know the true score on this.

Mannix: I appreciate your honesty, Mr. Brognola. I know you're taking a big chance coming here to tell me this.

Brognola: Thank you, Senator. I'll be in touch. I have to brief the President in fifteen minutes.

The secretary stopped transcribing the conversation at that point and hid her notes in her desk until Brognola left the office and the senator was back behind a closed door. She went to the fax machine, dialed a sensitive number that rang into FEMA headquarters and faxed her notes. Once the fax was sent, she put her shorthand notes into the paper shredder and then took the contents of the trash can down to the incinerator for immediate burning.

The opposition now had the wrong impression.

The Texas strike was on.

4

The Mecca America Travel State, Midland, Texas

He drew curious looks wherever he went inside the newest standard in roadside stops for the highway traveler and professional. The sun had already set, and darkness surrounded this island of light in the flat desert of the panhandle. The man's operative name was Mr. Saracino, and he'd already seen action in west Texas.

Saracino was SENSOPS, and his black clothing was distinctive. It was the four diamonds on his suit lapel that were getting all the whispers and the pointed fingers. The four diamonds signified the apex of attainment to a certain subsection of the marketing world known for cult behaviors and pie-in-the-sky claims to fortune.

It all amounted to the same thing: the world of counterintelligence, a world of smoke, mirrors and bluff. The rah-rah rally blowing the doors off the Alamo convention floor hosted by the Hi-SCI Nutriceutical Company was the bluff. It served as diversion and cover for the real operation in attendance: the COMCON command-cell summit that the top two floors of the twelve-floor tower were really devoted to.

The men in black were being touted as "the elite of Hi-SCI, the four-diamond distributor." None of the devotees of Hi-SCI seemed to notice that there were no one-, two- or three-diamond distributors walking around the area. None existed. Those slots in the pyramid existed only inside the Hi-SCI sponsorship "tool" that described the royalty payouts enjoyed at each level in the multilevel ladder to ultimate financial leverage. The devotees were more aware of the competing company blowing the doors off the Santa Ana convention floor with their own rah-rah rally right across the atrium from the Alamo. Agents provocateurs from both companies were already embroiling Mecca America convention management in disputes and counterdisputes over "noise" and other minor squabbles.

Saracino had been dispatched by his control to intercept whoever it was that was inbound in a chopper under radar with a transponder signal that checked out as one of theirs, but was otherwise a "ghost in the machine." No flight plans were available. Filed, but not available. No maintenance records. It was a bird that didn't seem to have a home port.

Very unusual, and it was raising some flags.

He exited the building and made his way out back to the LZ, to the edge of the double-football-field-sized lot, crossed the demarcation line into the desert and walked into the darkness until he was out of the circles of light.

He was invisible now. The helicopter, when it entered the LZ, wouldn't be noticed, as well. People didn't have much incentive anymore to pay attention. It was a mind-set being encouraged on purpose.

A voice was in his ear, a voice on a split-second delay as the built-in algorithm decrypted the transmission.

"Mr. Saracino, our inquiry on your inbound has been returned. You are to offer any support asked for by our guest. Our guest has executive action class 9 privileges."

Saracino whistled. "They must be bringing a new member into the Committee."

"Mr. Saracino, you are not paid to speculate as to the business of the Committee. You execute the will of the Committee. You do not examine it. Is that clear, Mr. Saracino?"

Saracino blushed in the darkness. Even when he was trying not to, he seemed to find a way to let his superiors know that he was still a pup. Saracino was still toiling under the oppressive shadow of his failure in May. The pictures of the AeroDeths had slipped through his net and landed on the cover of the July issue of *Soldier of Fortune* magazine.

Those sensitive photos had been taken by an Odessan named Homer Gump. Saracino had been assigned the job of killing the Gump family and getting those pictures back. His operation was a success when it came to killing the family, but Gump had pulled a switch, and the pictures ended up in the wrong hands.

Because of that faux pas, Saracino's career options had become severely limited.

He was lucky he was still wearing the elite black uniform of this secret corps. Look what happened to Newport. He could have ended up like that or worse. *Worse* in this case was being forced to swallow lead pain remedies. Yeah, right through the medulla oblongata at point-blank range.

These days, Saracino liked to lie low. He was happy being a good gofer who didn't make waves. His ambitions could wait until things blew over.

Saracino swallowed hard on his memories and answered, "A poor observation on my part, I submit."

"Good. You know your place and don't argue. You are going to do whatever our guest wants. Understood?"

"Yes."

"Now be a good little soldier. Follow orders. Don't question anything."

"Of course."

He'd keep his questions to himself.

"Don't make our detachment look incompetent."

"I'm waiting at the LZ."

"Keep me apprised."

"Of course."

The innuendo and acid comments were a cross to bear, and Saracino suffered quietly.

He thought about the mystery of the inbound agent and the guy's clearance level to act. Perhaps if Saracino could impress a guy like this, maybe the guy would say something good about him. It might help smooth things out for him.

Now he just had to make sure that he didn't come off like a pup.

THE TROOP DOOR SLID aside, and the big man in black jogged under the rotor wash with a black nylon duffel bag thrown over a shoulder. The bag looked heavy, filled with more than just an overnight change of clothes.

An updraft caught the guy's suit coat and flashed Saracino a look at the personal armory. There was a handgun under each arm, riding in shoulder rigs. The flash of shooting steel wasn't lasting enough for him to identify the weapons by make or caliber. He saw one weapon was silver in color, stainless or nickel plated; the other was matte black.

The big guy straightened to full height once he was out from under the whirling but remarkably quiet blades. He turned toward the pilot and made two gestures with his right hand: first a circle formed by the index finger and thumb, then index finger up and thumb tucked to make the number 1. It was a signal that only had meaning between the two of them.

In answer, the helicopter lifted off the ground and wagged left and right like a giant flying scorpion before pivoting toward the east and flying in that direction. The big guy turned and looked at Saracino.

"I like it when they send somebody to carry my bag," he said.

The big man threw the duffel into Saracino's unprepared arms. He almost dropped the bag but found some leverage somewhere that kept it out of the dirt.

"And I'm going to need a room. What's your name? Come on, come on. You don't want me to make something up."

"Ah, call me Saracino."

"I think I'm going to call you Herman Melville. You just about said the opening line to *Moby Dick* word for word."

The big man started to walk toward the lights and snapped his fingers over his shoulder. The sound was like a rifle crack.

"We don't have all night, Herman. Let's go. A sense of urgency, please. I've got very important business here tonight."

Saracino jogged to get ahead of the VIP, so he could lead the way in.

MACK BOLAN PLAYED his cards as they were dealt. His advance intel amounted to little more than studying satellite imagery of Mecca America's 110-acre square of west Texas, taken from low orbit, along with the blueprints Newport had provided on the disk. From the ground, things always looked different. Almost half the plot was slabbed over with concrete for parking. Most of that parking was devoted to semis and RVs. What wasn't available above ground for plain cars in parking space was found underground in one of three parking levels.

The place had just about everything under one roof

that could possibly be of interest to the weary traveler beat up by the road. Everything but a funeral home. By sunup, the place was going to need one.

Bolan's first priority was getting a feel for the lie of the battlefield. Identify targets and remove targets of opportunity as the situation dictated, find the brain cells, isolate them, then burn them off the planet like evil roaches, mop it up and exfil, while harming none of the other guests or even letting them get to see the color of the enemy's blood. It was a tall order.

The Executioner was legendary for feats of daring like this.

It always helped if his credit was good, too. His credit here amounted to his identity. It was his most important medium of exchange. His cover story was impressive. Newport had been very thorough in creating a bogus accounting of a SENSOPS "special" that never existed. Part of this exercise had to be a taunt, one blood opponent to the other. The devil was in the details. Newport had provided Bolan with bona fide SENSOPS identification and authentication algorithms so that Bolan could be at this gathering, walking among them as one of their own. The computerized files, copies of the same files that had been opened into the SENSOPS/FEMA personnel database, revealed an uncomfortable access to the classified details of Mack Bolan's covert life.

Bolan's cover name was Tony Donato. He was a SENSOPS "special," and had executive privilege within the parameters of the job. According to the jacket, Bolan's alter ego was a Black Ace once upon a time in Chicago, and when the Sicilian Mafia's stranglehold on American organized crime weakened and then crumbled, Donato became a free agent, selling his services to clients who could pay the price.

The price was high. Too high for most.

Walking across the acres of overnight semi parking in the cold light of giant halogen bulbs was making Saracino chatty.

"What do I call you, sir?"

"You got it right there. Call me 'sir.'"

The guy just blurted it out. "Is there going to be trouble here?"

"What makes you think that there could be trouble?"

"Your clearance to act. This bag. My back tells me it's full of weapons. And you look like some kind of specialist. A problem solver."

Bolan chuckled. "Yeah, I've solved some problems in my time. Now your guy, Newport, he wants me to solve his problems, too."

"Joe Newport fielded you? When?"

"How long's your trouble been going on?"

"What?"

"You know. That *guy* you and your people have been getting whacked by. How long's that been going on?"

A light seemed to be coming on in the smaller man's face.

"Oh. That guy. Yeah. Since May."

"There. You're the smart guy after all. You answered your own question."

"So you were brought in because of that guy."

Bolan nodded. "Yeah. I'm here because of that guy. You should be very glad that I got here first."

The confusion was back in the other man's face. "How's that?"

"Well, now I might have enough time to get you guys ready for when *he* gets here. Are you getting it yet?"

"He's coming here?"

"He might already be here. He won't budge until he knows who's who."

"But I heard he was dead, sir. Died yesterday morning in a raid."

"Maybe you heard wrong."

Saracino filed that information away without commenting.

"How did he find out about here?"

"First things first. Stopping him is my first job. Squeezing the canary is my second job. Where I come from, Herman, we have a long-standing tradition of chopping squealers and informants into dog food."

Bolan made sure that the two of them had real good eye contact.

"Make sure you don't ever look like dog food to me."

FELIX GOODS SHIELDED his eyes from flying gravel and debris as the AeroDeth touched down on the rooftop and Joe Newport emerged, dressed in the uniform of SENSOPS. As soon as Newport was off-loaded, the black helicopter took off again, heading west, going low.

Woods looked the former SENSOPS chief up and down.

"I heard black wasn't your color anymore. Mr. *Brown*."

Newport smiled menacingly. "The reign of my replacement is over. I'm back now."

"That's news I haven't heard."

"Go tell them I'm here. Tell them that I've vanquished their enemy for them. Bolan's dead, and I'm taking my place back."

MR. SARACINO WAS EXHAUSTED by the time he made it to the registration desk. He let go of the duffel bag, and it made an impressive thud on the polished black marble floor. As he stepped up to the desk to talk to the pretty, smiling blonde, the big guy yanked him back and around.

"I don't want a room with the rest of our crowd. Put me somewhere out of sight, you know? It's part of my plan to trap that guy."

"Ah, okay."

"And stay with that bag, Herman. Personally see that it gets to my room, then put somebody in there with it to guard it."

Saracino wanted to question these instructions.

"Ah, okay."

"In the meantime, I want to have a quiet look at your security. No warnings that I'm coming, Herman.

I want to see your boys doing what they're normally doing when they know nobody is watching."

"This is a pretty tight operation."

"Sure. They're all tight when there's an inspection, somebody watching who needs impressing. I haven't seen a well-oiled machine yet that's well oiled around the clock. That's my point."

"Ah, okay."

"If you need me, have the hotel page me."

"Okay, but…"

"Donato. Tony Donato, kid. Have them say something like 'Mr. Donato, we found your blonde.' Then I'll know it's you and that you want something."

Saracino had to repeat it. "Mr. Donato, we found your blonde."

"You got it, kid. I think you're learning how to play along with Tony. So you know what I expect, right?"

"Yes. I think I do."

"So where are we, Herman? In the building?"

"Oh. Top two floors—we own them. The Committee is working out of the penthouse. We've got agents scattered all over in between keeping an eye on all entry vectors."

"Entry vectors, huh? I like that."

"You might be impressed with what you see out there."

"I'm usually not," he said, then turned, walking quickly for the stairwell door.

THE KEY TO role camouflage was staying in front of your opponents' thought processes, give them answers to their questions before they could wonder about the questions, and do this from a position of perceived status within the pack hierarchy. If the operative had the bravado and sheer intestinal fortitude to pull these feats from deep inside, then chances were the locals would be fooled for a while. Hopefully, for long enough to do the job right.

Bolan hit the door to the stairwell and took the concrete steps two at a time. The walls, landings and stairs were painted the same dark shade of battleship gray. The floor numbers were painted in red inside white circles on the back of each stairwell door, which was the same authoritarian shade of gray as the walls and floors.

Bolan's plan right now was to go up.

He found one of the MIBs loitering on the landing of the third floor, pacing with his arms crossed. The guy tensed, but seeing Bolan's black suit, shirt and tie caused him to make an association that wasn't at all accurate.

The Executioner wasn't a friendly.

Bolan nodded up at the guy as he left the landing, mounting the last flight up to three.

"Hey, comrade, if you see someone who looks like me," Bolan said, pausing as the 93-R materialized in his right fist, "kill him!"

The guy frantically tried to reach the concealed P-38 as a pencil line of flame licked the distance between the muzzle dot and the red dot that magically appeared on the guy's forehead. The lights winked out and the body collapsed. Bolan calmly gained the higher landing and relieved the corpse of the tac radio. He tucked the small black box inside his breast pocket and stuck the earpiece in his left ear.

The guy two landings above came to life. The stairwell was a natural amplifier, and the suppressor on the 93-R wasn't magic. There was still a muzzle-blast on the weapon. A greatly reduced one, granted, but still louder than a child's cap gun. That sharp crack echoed up the concrete shaft, followed immediately by that unmistakable sound as a body dropped to cold concrete. Bolan heard the soft treads as the guy two landings up descended cautiously to see what was going on.

Bolan catfooted back down to two. He yanked the door open on the landing and popped onto the floor. Two more of the MIBs were stationed at the elevator alcove midway down the hall. One was seated reading a betting sheet, and the other was leaning into the wall like bracing.

"Hey, you limp pricks! I got a man down in here! Shots fired, man! Let's move!"

The two MIBs went into action mode, lurching to their feet and drawing side arms as they hurried toward Bolan.

"What's going on?"

"Man down next floor up! We've got a security breach!"

Bolan let the two go up in front of him. The Desert Eagle hand cannon was pulled out of reserve and filled the Executioner's left fist. He mounted the stairs calmly, following the two agents.

The man on five was on the landing now, and the other two made three armed and very edgy targets.

"Jesus, it's Franz," one of the men said.

One of the two on elevator detail turned toward Bolan. "Did you see who did this?"

Bolan nodded. "Yeah, I did it."

The Executioner caught them flatfooted. He leveled both handguns and opened fire. The .44 Magnum round in the enclosed space was like naval gunfire. The soft-nose boattail slug hit the man from the fifth floor in the hollow of his shoulder, punching him off his feet backward into the concrete wall. The back of his head made a squished-melon sound, smacking off the wall, and he collapsed to the floor, permanently out of the play. The Beretta coughed twice for the elevator detail, bang-on head shots destroying their skulls.

The enemy tac net became a bedlam of traffic. The ringing of the Magnum round was still reverberating up and down the stairwell like a concrete gong. The sentries in the stairwell above five were pounding down the stairs without trying to be quiet.

Bolan took to their net. "All stations! All stations! Hold in place! This is Donato! I'm in the stairwell, too! I was right under him!"

The guys coming down the stairs were almost on him.

Bolan yelled, "Hey, listen to the radio, meatheads! I said, hold in place!"

One of those men up above yelled back, "What the fuck's going on?"

"This is Donato. We have a situation in the stairwell. I need cool right now, people. Our guy is on three or four. We need to keep a ceiling intact. That's why the dumb bastards in the stairwell need to stay high, not low! We don't want this boy getting above us. We want to put him in a sandwich now.

"Herman, are you keeping up with this, kid?"

SARACINO WAS GLAD that none of his superiors were on hand to see his performance.

Jumping around in circles using hopping steps, facing every which way, trying in vain to pin down the direction that the sound of the shot had come from. He remembered his weapon and fumbled for it. The central atrium was arcing off nervous energy as milling groups pointed all around, looking for the source of the gunshot.

Then Donato was giving instructions over the net, and Saracino froze to hang on every word.

"Herman, are you keeping up with this, kid?"

Herman Melville—that was Saracino. Donato was trying to talk to him.

"Yeah! Mr. Donato! I'm here!"

"He's here, kid. I need you to find management and keep this stairwell off limits and lock the elevators down on one. You got that, kid?"

Saracino was marveling at Donato's ability to make such subtle adjustments in the heat of battle.

"Yes, I've got it!"

"Then do it!"

Saracino dived at the counter. It was time to play *federale*. The blonde at the desk was fumbling with the phone, trying to call 911.

"I'm a federal agent! Get the manager immediately!"

5

It was less a conference and more a pageant. It was a holiday for them, the sons of Nazi Germany. It was a yearly tradition since 1963. To the COMCON secret history, November 22 was like the Fourth of July to most other Americans. Both dates were birthday celebrations. By November 22, 1963, the sons of Nazi Germany owned the U.S. intelligence and covert ops capability in every way that mattered. President Kennedy was of a mind to set things back on the proper course inside U.S. intelligence, which amounted to rooting out all the Nazi blood that was in its second generation and working on its third by then.

President Kennedy never had the chance.

On November 22, 1963, the sons of Nazi Germany quietly took over the executive branch of government in the U.S.A. The assassination was part of the classic coup d'état without all the major political upheaval. The legislative and judicial branches played look-the-other-way and generally followed lockstep right behind the executive branch in the silent transition to secret fascism.

This covert cabal had come to expect success as a

matter of course. Since the relocation at the end of the big war, the march toward the global reich had encountered few serious setbacks. It always came as something of a shock when a venture didn't go their way. However, even the setbacks were always temporary. Any bump on the road merely required proper application of a road grader to "smooth" things out. If a problem couldn't be bought, seduced or evangelized, the problem was terminated. Terminated delicately and as quietly as possible. If quiet couldn't be managed, then the megaviolence was contracted out of house, and the results were still the same.

The march went forward.

And they were one step closer to the Thousand-Year Reich.

Mack Bolan wasn't a speed bump on the road to the Fourth Reich. Bolan was a death sentence. He unwound tentacles and crushed dark dreams.

When it all came down to a profit-and-loss statement, Mack Bolan spelled the difference between taking it all or losing everything. The Bolan effect could be counted on to place big numbers into the loss columns, compounded daily.

If the Fourth Reich was to flourish, a man like Bolan couldn't be tolerated.

In the end, survival came down to one thing: men like Bolan had to die. There could never be a middle ground, a truce. The world just wasn't big enough.

Bolan died or the dream of the reich died.

There were some things that couldn't be done quietly.

THE EXECUTIVE ACTION committee of COMCON was composed of three cells: A, B and C. While cell A was composed of three men, cells B and C each had five members. All planning and decision-making was handed down from A cell, the command cell, B and C cells were action cells. They made things happen. Together, these thirteen men were the brains, eyes and ears of COMCON, the Committee to suspend the Constitution. The membership roster read like a who's who of the nation's most powerful and important men.

Each cell had a commander.

Brent Dunphy, code name Number 12, commanded A cell. Dunphy had a day job as a high-ranking member of the National Security Agency. He had access to anything the U.S. intelligence community was privy to know, and he was directly responsible for directing and overseeing the activities of C cell.

Cell A's number-two man was Admiral James D. Corr, code name Spartacus. Corr was a member of the Joint Chiefs of Staff. His influence spread through all branches of the military and into the boardrooms of America's most influential defense contractors.

Up until his unfortunate demotion, Joe Newport had been the third member of the command cell. Newport was the chief of SENSOPS, the men in black, who were the heart and soul of the rogue federal agency FEMA. FEMA was poised to run the entire country from the top down once any one of COMCON's subversion ops was successful in placing the country in a state of national emergency and martial law.

William Laforge, deputy director of Intelligence for the CIA, commanded B cell. Laforge's code name was Methuselah. He directed the activities of the other four members of B cell. Henry Klinger, code name Lexington, was the undersecretary of state and member of the National Security Council. Todd Turner, code name Concord, was the U.S. Ambassador to the United Nations. Oscar Batt, code name Patriot, was the deputy director of the FBI. Luther Gehlen was the diehard link right back to Nazi Germany. Gehlen was the leader of ODESSA, the organization of veterans of the SS. His code name was Father.

Bush Wainwright commanded C cell. He was the president of Yale University. His code name was Dreamer. Steven Reinhard was Hollywood's biggest director and filmmaker of all time. His company, the Wish Factory, was responsible for some of the most incredible special-effects extravaganzas ever produced. His code name was Optimist. Dr. Jonathan Duke was the director of the FDA and was spearheading the drive to place all nutrient supplements into the category of drugs, which would effectively crush the alternative-medicine movement and severely curtail longevity research. His code name was Narcissus. Mr. Mason Jefferson was the patriarch of the oldest banking family in America. He sat at the helm of the Jefferson family flagship, Jefferson Manhattan Bank. He was also a special adviser to the Federal Reserve board of governors. His code name was

Goldwater. Ernest Morreese was the green subversive marrying the New Age to the environmental movement. He was the founder of the Moongreen Party, a weird amalgamation of militant paganism and green politics. He sat on the board of directors of the Sierra Club and was a high-ranking delegate at the UN Convention on the Rights of the Earth. His code name was Evergreen.

Each member of the executive committee was responsible for developing and directing cells of their own within their spheres of influence and areas of expertise. The roots and tentacles of this core cadre ran deep and touched the lives of millions of people.

Roman passions and excess hadn't died with Imperial Rome. A secret society was formed beneath the conquering Christians and the good times rolled— good times based on the premise that a few were born to run and exploit everyone else. This kind of fun had a price tag in flesh and blood.

The *need* was everything. Economics and breeding separated the royalty from the serfs. It was birthright that legitimized rape and oppression. The elite could do as they pleased. The elite were godlings. The masses were fodder. Circumstances of birth and inheritance would be the new currency on this global plantation, the criteria by which men were judged for worth, merit and privilege. It would be the new feudalism. No more middle class or upwardly mobile. There would be the haves and the have-nots. There were too many have-nots reproducing like rats in the world, and the fascist world order would cull these masses like cattle, cutting them back to manageable levels.

The coming Holocaust would be orchestrated in the name of Mother Earth. Genocide by reason of race or belief was passe. The climate was ripe for the slaughter of billions in the name of protecting the environment from the human "plague." Of course, only Third World countries bursting at the seams with overpopulation and "mud races" would suffer the worst of the killing. So it still was a race thing when all the green propaganda was scrubbed away to reveal the nature of this beast.

The heart of Nazi Germany was still beating strong.

IT WAS A GALA DISCO BALL in the penthouse. Loud music and the best drugs.

The penthouse occupied the entire twelfth floor, thirteen thousand square feet of creature comforts. The kitchen was all chrome and polished oak. There were three bedroom suites, each with a private bath and whirlpool. The living room-den was the biggest part of the floor plan. There was a fully stocked wet bar with enough space for ten people to belly up for drinks. The outlying floor space was raised above the center level, which was dominated by a hardwood dance floor. A billiard table was off to one side of the room, while the huge entertainment center dominated the opposite end. A formal dining room was built off the kitchen.

The party raged in the living room-den. The place had the atmosphere of a high-dollar strip joint: blinking colored lights and mirrored balls. The twelve most powerful men in the country sat and watched the show on the dance floor.

The emcee of the night's festivities was an important person to these men, although he didn't hold an executive post in the conspiracy. He was a pawn but a very valued one. He was dressed in shades of gunmetal gray, tweed sport coat and a black turtleneck. His name was Gabriel Aquarius, a turkey doctor of the mind.

He was hosting what amounted to a white-slave auction. Every year he came before these men and offered them the cream of his work at a premium price. Each of these men kept private stables in remote locations for their sex slaves. Every year the stables were replenished, while the previous year's models were all shipped to a private ranch in Wyoming where the Most Dangerous Game was played out. The previous year's playthings were this year's hunt. The young women were turned loose naked and barefoot with instructions to run, while these men dressed in shooting jackets and breeches like aristocracy on a foxhunt. The women were hunted down and shot like game animals.

He had twenty-four young women with him this night, and they all did the same circuit.

A young woman would round the corner, staying on the upper level, strutting provocatively while maintaining smoky eye contact with the "johns." She'd hop up on the pool table and bust out a raunchy grind of a dance, then jump down and hit the dance floor. The dance became even raunchier down on the floor, then the girl would do the circuit through the crowd like a real pro. The circuit was completed back in the bedroom for a wardrobe change.

This would go on until the wee hours of the morning, until these high-powered bull elks of depravity were so high and drunk that they couldn't contain themselves any longer. The orgy would last past dawn, then the men would make their choices and the money would change hands. After that, Aquarius never saw the young women again, and he didn't care what became of them. He went back to work and made more human automatons. He loved the process of breaking down the human mind with trauma and rebuilding the personality to fit his own twisted specifications.

It was more than a science. It was art of the most esoteric order.

Aquarius was a master chef, and this gala was his smorgasbord.

The front door to the penthouse suite opened without notice. Felix Woods stepped into the entryway and Newport came in behind him. The self-reinstated SENSOPS chief stepped around Woods like a minor obstacle on the road to bigger things.

"Goddammit, Newport!" Woods yelled, "I've got to announce you."

Newport flipped the guy a bird over his shoulder and continued into the suite.

Woods tried to stop him, which was a mistake. In full view of the executive committee, Newport swatted the hands off his shoulders, slammed the man into the wall and stuck the barrel of his own P-38 into his face.

"You're taking orders from me now. Do you understand? I'm back. And that's all that needs to be said."

Woods couldn't decide what was more menacing—the weapon in his face or the fire in Newport's eyes. He decided to keep his mouth shut and let the Committee decide who was in charge here. All eyes in the room were now on Newport and the gun he pointed into Woods's face.

Brent Dunphy, the A cell commander, walked up slowly. He had a brotherly smile on his face, but his eyes were cold-blooded and reptilian.

"Joe?" he said. "What do you have this man's gun in his face for? What are you wearing that suit for? You're not the chief anymore, Joe."

"Fuck you, Brent."

Those eyes flared with anger, but the voice remained calm and cordial.

"Let's talk about this, Joe. We'll see what we can figure out."

"Turn that fucking music off!" Newport yelled. "And get these bitches out of here! The pussy parade is over!"

Nobody in the room moved. The hard stares stayed on Newport and the girls kept dancing, working the crowd.

Newport spun and fired one thundering round into the stereo system. The sudden quiet was deafening.

Then he turned back to his insubordinate subordinate and told him, "Get the fuck out of here, Woods. You're no longer required."

Woods hesitated. He looked at Dunphy for guidance. The man nodded.

"Go ahead, Mr. Woods. We'll handle this from here."

Woods jerked himself out of Newport's grasp, straightened his jacket and exited the penthouse.

"I don't know what your game is, Joe, but—"

Newport cut him off. "That's right, you don't know shit. But I'm here to enlighten you all."

Dunphy chuckled. "Okay, Joe. I get it. You're not happy with your sudden demotion. But you failed us. You have to be taught a lesson."

"School's out now, Brent. I redid my lesson plan. And this time, I got it right."

Dunphy just looked at him, boring hot eyes into Newport's. Newport didn't flinch or blink.

"Do you watch the news, Brent? Do any of you fucks watch the news anymore? No, I suppose not when you have all these sluts to be shacking up with. The business of this thing of ours can't quite compete with the pussy, can it?"

"What about the news?" Luther Gehlen asked.

"I'm talking about the *training* accident yesterday in Virginia. That terrible instant replay of the Desert One disaster. Delta Force and Army Special Operations Aviation crashing all their birds into that remote farm in Virginia. They actually broadcast pictures of that bastard's compound on the news. It was a pathetic attempt at a cover story, but the dumb fucks in this country have swallowed it hook, line and sinker.''

"Yes, I watch the news, Mr. Newport," Gehlen said. "Everybody died in that accident. Which leaves me to wonder why you are still alive."

Newport grinned like a shark. "I was demoted, remember? I had to stay behind while the glorious attack went forward. It went forward, all right. My replacement is dead, but so is our nemesis. He died there. I confirmed it myself."

"How did you do that, Joe?" Dunphy asked. "If you were a stay-behind, I mean?"

"You need to pay closer attention to operations manifests, Brent. We went out there with fourteen birds, not thirteen. The extra bird stayed behind in reserve, in case something went wrong."

William Laforge remarked, "Yes, something did go wrong. There was a mysterious fire at Camp Perry that night. Several of our troops were killed. What do you know about that, Joe?"

Newport used the man's code name in vain. "You really must be getting as old and as senile as Methuselah, Bill, because you just aren't as sharp as a tack anymore. What do you think happened? Huh? Those throwaways weren't going to let me leave."

"You killed them?"

"Yeah, I killed them."

"And then you took the reserve helicopter and flew out to the target area."

Newport nodded. "Exactly. I got there as it was ending. I helped end it by mopping up the rest of that bastard's security forces. I walked through that carnage until I found him. He was dead in the big house with half his head blown off.''

"You sure it was him?"

"I'm the only one in this organization who met this bastard face-to-face and lived to tell about it. Yeah, it was him. It was Mack Bolan.''

Newport could see that Admiral James D. Corr was watching him very intently, maintaining eye contact whenever possible.

"Take a fuckin' picture, Admiral," Newport snarled. "It lasts longer.''

The admiral laughed. "You really are hell-bent for leather to piss off just about everybody in this room, aren't you, Newport?''

"This is just tit for tat, Admiral.''

"Oh, sure, son. I can see that.''

"Do you have something to contribute, or are you just sounding off?''

"Well, your story does seem to have independent confirmation.'' He looked at Dunphy. "Doesn't it, Brent?''

Dunphy looked at the admiral and nodded reluctantly.

"Sure, it does.''

Newport gazed from one man to the other, waiting for some elaboration.

"Well, are you going to let me in on this?''

The admiral elected himself the storyteller. "A White House flunky—what's his name, Brent?''

"Harold Brognola.''

"Yes. Harold Brognola. He paid a visit to the office of Senator John Mannix yesterday afternoon. He went there to notify our dear senator that his favorite attack dog had been put to sleep. The senator's secretary keeps an eye on him for us. She made a transcript in shorthand of their conversation. This Brognola confirms that Bolan is dead, as you claim he is."

Newport had to laugh. He couldn't have orchestrated it any better himself.

"Well, I can see right now that this bullshit interrogation can stop right here! You have confirmation beyond a doubt that I'm telling the truth here. So let's cut the shit and make this official. My replacement is fertilizer, and I'm taking my place back."

Newport made a point of displaying the fact that he was still holding the gun.

"I'm not taking no for an answer, either."

Newport didn't care what they thought of his thinly veiled threat. They were all going to be dead by dawn anyway. Then he'd do in Bolan for real, and the entire network would be his to direct. The world would be his oyster.

Dunphy finally broke the awkward silence.

"As always, Joe, you've proved you're a man who makes things happen."

"You're goddamn right I am."

"You've never failed us in the past. Not until Bolan came along."

Bush Wainwright, commander of C cell, added, "This maniac Bolan has made monkeys of the best. The entire Sicilian Mafia couldn't shut down this one man. Perhaps we need to give Mr. Newport a little clemency.''

''I say we reinstate this man,'' the admiral suggested.

Dunphy held out his hand. ''Welcome back to SENSOPS, Joe.''

Newport took the offered hand and shook it. The two men smiled at each other warmly, but their eyes were stone cold dead. Newport knew he'd have to kill Dunphy almost immediately. He could see that just by looking into the guy's eyes. Dunphy was going to have him killed otherwise. The chief of SENSOPS had pushed the envelope way too far this time.

Everyone else seemed to know these facts, as well. The reinstatement was going to be temporary. It would buy the time necessary to engineer Newport's permanent retirement. In the eyes of his peers, Newport wasn't just disrespectful and insubordinate. He was a loose cannon to boot.

The front door banged open and Felix Woods practically sprinted back into the Committee's midst.

''There's trouble,'' he announced. ''Four of our men have been killed on three. The south stairwell.''

A ripple of shock moved through the assembled brain cells of COMCON. Several of the men got up from their seats and moved into the edges of the huge party pad, nervously eyeing and staying away from the bay of floor-to-ceiling windows.

Newport took this as his cue to take charge.

''Who's in charge down there, Woods?''

Woods glared at Newport and didn't answer, looking to Dunphy for direction.

"He's the chief again, Mr. Woods. At least for now he is."

The import of the A cell commander's last statement wasn't lost on Newport.

"What's going on down there, Woods? Who's in charge?"

The MIB's demeanor changed immediately. He stood straighter and looked directly to his front while rattling off his report.

"A new arrival, sir. A specialist with level 9 clearance. Somebody named Donato."

Newport nodded. "Yes. He's my special recruit."

Woods dropped the bombshell. "He thinks that Mack Bolan is here. Sir."

Had there been a gas leak in there, the sudden electrified mood could have sparked an explosion. The general ambience of the room became collectively grim. Now they were all looking around nervously.

Laforge growled, "What's going on here, Newport? Is this bastard dead or not?"

"It's not Bolan! I want that rumor squelched now!"

"Well, somebody killed four of our people," Dunphy said. "Who the hell is it?"

Newport's mind raced. "Bolan had a crew. One or two of them might be here now, trying to get some revenge."

Laforge voiced what had to have been on the other

men's minds. "How did Bolan's crew find out where we'd be?"

Newport whirled on the man and pointed an accusing finger at him.

"It's *your* agency that's got that bunch of patriotic rebels running hog wild through the hallowed halls of national security, Bill! What do they call themselves? The Fifth Column or some shit? They've been feeding Bolan intel since this started in May! If the leak is anywhere, it's coming out of your fucking agency, not mine, you son of a bitch!"

"Perhaps we should be coming together on this rather than biting each other's heads off," Bush Wainwright said. "Don't you think that this is what our opponents want, whoever they are? If they succeed in dividing us, they will win."

"Exactly correct," the admiral said. "This bickering has to stop."

Newport nodded in agreement. "Fuckin' A right. And I'm in charge of security here, which means I'm in charge now. None of you are to leave this floor. Is that clear? Until I have a clearer picture of what we're up against, all of you are restricted to the penthouse. I have an air asset standing by. If I have to, I can have every one of you airlifted out of here from the roof."

He turned to address Woods. "I need a radio, Woods. Give me yours."

The man nodded and pulled the earpiece out of his left ear and unclipped the radio from his belt. He handed the radio to Newport.

"Can I have my weapon back, sir?"

Newport looked blankly at the MIB, then handed the P-38 back to him.

"You're going to be on report for letting me take that away from you, Woods."

"Yes, sir."

"Listen up. I want more of our people up here covering the elevator and the roof. I want the penthouse and the eleventh floor completely locked down. And get some more weapons up here. I want every one of these prima donnas armed."

"Yes, sir."

"Move out, Woods."

The men nearly ran out of the room. Newport clipped the radio to his belt and put the earpiece in his ear. He turned his gaze to Gabriel Aquarius, who had been standing quietly throughout the interruption of his pageant.

"Aquarius, put your pussies on ice somewhere, okay? There's going to be no orgies tonight. The last thing I need is for Bolan's crew to bust in here and catch all of you with your pants around your ankles."

"Gabriel, the girls stay," Dunphy added. "Put them in the bedrooms. Half of us can have a little fun while the other half stays alert."

Newport shrugged. "Whatever, Brent. One of these days, you're going to let your *big* head start making some decisions around here."

With that, Newport headed out. It felt damn good getting the last poke in.

6

The tower was shaped like a big rectangle with twenty rooms on each floor. A stairwell was on each end of the oblong box, north and south sides, and double elevators were located in the center. The hallway cut the floor in two with ten rooms on each side. Each floor had an ice and snack room, laundry and linen storage for housekeeping. The laundry chute into the basement was located in the linen storage room. Each guest suite had a private balcony.

The Executioner holstered his weapons before opening the door on the landing and catfooting onto the third floor. Three was clear. No one was milling around. Bolan quickly covered the length of the hallway, pausing along the way to poke his head inside the door marked Housekeeping. No maids were present, just shelves of linens and toiletries. He pulled his head out of the storage room and continued the rest of the way down the hall to the opposite stairwell.

He opened the door carefully and stepped through. There was another MIB in the stairwell on the landing and the guy slapped leather on Bolan as soon as he appeared through the doorway. Bolan immediately raised his hands.

"Hey, guy! Wait a minute! I'm Donato."

The man lowered his P-38 and relaxed a notch, but the guy was still wound as tight as a watch spring.

"What the hell's going on?"

"We've got a shooter. Four guys down already on the other side. You haven't seen anybody, have you?"

"Hell no. Just you."

Bolan feigned disgust.

"Goddammit. He *has* to be on this floor. He's gotta be hiding, then. Come on."

"What?"

"We're going to check out this floor."

"Just the two of us? Maybe we should call for some backups."

"Yeah, that'd be a good idea. But the guys higher up need to stay there. We don't need this son of a bitch getting through."

"You think you know who it is?"

"Yeah. I think it's Bolan."

"No shit? I heard he got his check cashed yesterday."

"Maybe. Maybe not. That guy has more lives than a cat."

The MIB realized Bolan didn't have a weapon in his hand. This seemed completely insane to him.

"Don't you have a gun?"

"Sure. I've got two."

"Well, shit! Why don't you have it out?"

Bolan shrugged. "I don't want to startle the guests."

"Jesus! Fuck the guests! If Bolan's here, on this floor like you think, we're going to need more guns!"

"Yeah, yeah. Come on."

Bolan turned and went back through the door onto the third floor. His new partner followed him warily, checking every corner and obstruction in view that a man could possibly hide behind. He had his P-38 out in front of him at full extension the whole time, in a two-fisted grip. His eyes were open wide with trepidation.

Bolan went to the housekeeping door again and got to one side of the door. He nodded at his partner.

"Cover me."

The MIB got out of the line of fire to the other side and covered the door. Bolan reached out and twisted the knob, shoving the door open. He went in low around the jamb, pulling the 93-R free as he did so. He made a show of checking things out while his partner stayed to the rear. Bolan dug through the piled laundry inside a big canvas-sided cart. Nothing.

Bolan straightened and really put on a play of looking miffed.

"There's just not too many goddamn places he can hide around here."

"Maybe he's got a room. Did you think about that?"

"Maybe we should just call the front desk and see if there's a Mack Bolan registered in this hotel."

The MIB got the drift that he was being stupid. He didn't offer any more suggestions.

Bolan considered the hatch to the laundry chute, then frowned. He motioned to the door with a wave of the suppressor.

"Hey, check out the chute."

"Why?"

"Listen, this guy is no rank amateur. He's probably brought all kinds of James Bond shit with him, like suction-cup climbing gear. He could be in that chute just stuck to the side walls like some kind of frigging human fly! Nobody'd think to look in there for him. Check it out."

"Why me? You're closer."

"Yeah, but who went through the door first? It's your goddamn turn."

The MIB grumbled but reluctantly strolled over to the hatch and warily opened it.

The guy made a cursory peek through the hatch without actually sticking his head into the chute.

"Looks clear."

"He's not going to be hanging right inside the hatch, dumb-ass! Stick your head in there!"

The MIB stuck his gun hand in first, waved it around a few seconds, clanging against the sheet metal walls. When nobody opened fire on him, he decided it was probably safe and stuck his head in for a look-see.

It was safe in there. The real danger was standing right behind the guy.

The MIB started to report. "It's clear—"

The suppressor coughed behind him, and a 9 mm chunk of nonsurgical metal severed communication between the brain and the spinal column at the base of the skull. The guy dropped like a sack of manure and got hung up in the hatch, hanging by his chin in the L of the square opening. The P-38 clattered to the floor. The guy's legs and arms kicked spastically for a few seconds as the bladder involuntarily emptied against the wall.

Death was never a pretty event, and Bolan felt a momentary twinge about doing the guy like that.

War was about winning, not about being fair.

Bolan pulled a big canvas laundry bag off one of the shelves and unfolded it with a hard flick of his wrist. He pulled the bag up over the dead man's legs, then over the body up to the torso, tightening the cotton drawstrings and tying them down. Then he took a second laundry bag, lifted the body out of the opening by the back collar and wrapped a few dirty sheets around the head to soak up the blood before he pulled the sack over the corpse's head. He tied down the second drawstring, then heaved the body into the shoot headfirst.

The body made a hellish banging on the metal walls throughout the free fall. Bolan closed the hatch. With any luck, the body wouldn't be discovered until after his business here was finished.

The Executioner exited the room and went back to the hunt.

JOE NEWPORT TOOK the stairs down from the penthouse and passed by several of his men who were guarding the landing. He acted as if they weren't there. As he jogged from landing to landing, he went over the net with his announcement.

"All SENSOPS personnel. This is your leader, Joe Newport, speaking. The once and current chief. I am not happy with the way I've been treated since arriving in Texas. Some people in this organization seem to think my name is still Mr. Brown. I'm going to say this once. Tristan Zeigler is dead. I am running this organization again. Woe be unto the next guy who questions me, back talks me or mad dogs me. I will shoot that guy on sight, and don't think I won't. Everyone acknowledge what I just said."

The SENSOPS net came to life as the agents began to acknowledge what Newport just said.

Newport didn't know how many of his people were on hand in the hotel to provide security for the gathering. He'd figure that out after taking care of the bodies in the stairwell.

"Outstanding. Next order of business is rumor control. I understand somebody is dropping hints that Mack Bolan is crashing our party tonight. I repeat, like Zeigler, Mack Bolan is dead. If anybody is on the loose here, it's probably one of Bolan's crew, looking for revenge. Keep your eyes open and stay in groups."

Newport was on five when the stairwell door burst open and an older man in a hotel blazer armed with a walkie-talkie crowded onto the landing.

"I'm investigating the gunshot now," the hotel detective told somebody over the walkie-talkie.

Newport punched the man back onto the fifth floor and pinned him against a wall.

"You're not investigating shit, old man. There was no gunshot, got it? I'm a federal operative and so is everybody else that looks like I do. We're covering this, which means you can go back to sneaking into women's rooms and stealing their dirty panties. Are we clear on that?"

The old guy nodded.

"Ye-ye-yes, sir."

Newport let go of him.

"Actually, you can do me a favor. I'm deputizing you. Just stand on this side of the door, okay, and make sure nobody goes in that stairwell. Can you handle that, Deputy Dog?"

The hotel detective nodded again. "Yes, sir. I can do that, surely I can."

"Outstanding. If your pinhead manager tries to tell you different, you just tell him to fuck off because you're working for the Feds now. Got it?"

"Yes, sir."

Newport hit the stairwell again. He went back on the tac net with more detailed instructions.

"I need some of you lazy fucks on eleven to unhinge your asses from your chairs and get the hell in the south stairwell. I need coverage from five all the way down to the basement. Anybody not wearing black gets thrown out until we're done with the trash detail. I want to hear some shoe leather pounding these stairs now!"

Seven floors overhead, Newport was rewarded with the sound of the stairwell door crashing into the concrete wall and half a dozen sets of Oxford shoes running down after him.

Yeah, that was more like it. These guys were snapping and popping again. Thank God he hadn't been out of the driver's seat long enough for that asshole Zeigler to have totally thrown brutal discipline out the window.

These men were modern SS. They were going to act like it and be proud.

When he got to three, there were four of his boys on the landing looking down at the four dead. Three of the dead sported neat 9 mm holes in their foreheads. The other dead guy had his arm amputated at the shoulder and had died from shock and blood loss.

Newport didn't waste any time gawking.

"Let's get this shit cleaned up. I want this place looking forensics proof in five minutes or less! Find a maid's closet and get some sheets to wrap these bodies in. Find a mop and a bucket and lots of pine solvent and get this blood up. Get these bodies up on eleven. Get them in a nice big tub and put the acid on them. Make them disappear down the fuckin' drain."

The boys on door detail came around and went by, dropping off one guy at door number three while the others went leaping down the stairs to cover two, one and the basement.

As his men went to work on that task, Newport went down to the landing between three and two. He pulled the rumpled pack of cigarettes out of his breast pocket, shook one out and lit up. It had been hours since he last had a cigarette, and he hadn't really missed anything.

He thought about quitting again.

THE RED 1993 Corvette screeched off the highway and onto the concrete-covered acres of the Mecca America plot. The low road-hugging roadster cut through the gassing islands and into the parking area for cars. The Vette came to a smoking halt and took two open spaces at a diagonal cant. The quintessential American sports car got into the spaces just seconds before an ancient Oldsmobile station wagon with the gaudy simulated-wood side panels. There were no other open spaces up front, and the driver of the Oldsmobile began honking the horn like a lunatic.

The driver of the Vette didn't care. She was on a mission.

The woman was tall with a body like the huntress. She wore a one-piece black bodysuit made out of stretch fabric, black aerobics shoes and a jaunty red beret on top of her blond head. She pulled a black nylon athletic bag out of the Vette and slammed the door, locking it.

A very hostile overweight man leaned out the window of the Olds, screaming and honking.

"You dumb bitch! You can't take two spaces like that!"

It was the *B*-word that did it. She pivoted and walked over to the driver of the Olds. She reached out and grabbed his earlobe and nearly twisted it off his head. The fat man started to scream, then the fat woman next to him and the two fat kids in the back seat were screaming, as well.

"Don't call me a bitch, pig man," she said dangerously. "I'm not in the mood tonight."

He tried to yelp something that would appease her and stop the pain. She cranked it on for another second and then let go.

"And if I come back and find my car fucked up, I'll find you and cut your cock off and shove it down your fat throat in a goddamn hot dog bun."

"You're a fuckin' crazy bitch!"

"What did I say about calling me a bitch!"

She reached out to put the squeeze on him again, but the fat man was motivated to stay out of reach. He slammed the transmission into reverse and floored the accelerator. The Olds station wagon shot off backward doing at least thirty miles per hour on smoking treads. That land-locked torpedo jackhammered straight through the nose of a white Dodge Ram pickup with steer horns mounted on the hood. The pickup was coming through the cross lane nose first and spun three-sixty after the impact, crashing into another row of parked cars. The Olds was deflected by the crash and went diagonal across the lane into the cars parked on the opposite side. Hubcaps flew in all directions and the steer horns spun on the pavement like a top.

Her name was Lauren Hunter, and she finally had a reason to smile. She turned her back on that sorry sight, taking long-legged strides away from there and had a good belly laugh as she crossed the lot to the main entrance of the hotel.

"That'll teach you to call me a bitch, you fat bastard," she said to herself.

She walked through the glass entrance and went straight past the registration desk. She wasn't there for a room; she was there for revenge. Her best intelligence sources were all saying the same thing: Striker was dead. The Nazi bastards had brought him down in Virginia. The secret base in the Blue Ridge was in shambles. America's best defense was gone forever.

It infuriated her. It wasn't right that it had played out like that.

She knew where she'd find them.

Hunter was going to do them like he would have. Straight up the center with hellfire. She had some real goodies packed in that athletic bag, and she couldn't wait to use them. She unzipped the bag about six inches, just enough to put her hand inside and clutch the butt of the Ruger .22 pistol. The weapon was modified to be the perfect assassination tool. The entire barrel assembly had been removed and modified to be one long suppressor tube. This weapon truly was silenced. With the custom subsonic ammo, all the noise this little killer made was the sound of the action cycling the next round.

She spotted the stairwell door and adjusted her

course. The door banged open and she bulled into the stairwell. The MIB standing guard on the other side was just as surprised to see her as she was to see him. Hunter reacted immediately, jerking to the left while trying to tug the Ruger free of the bag.

The MIB shouted a warning as the door swung shut with a metallic click.

She pulled the Ruger free just as the MIB crashed into her, and the two of them were propelled by momentum into the concrete wall, the jaunty beret falling off her head. Frantic footfalls were coming from both directions in the stairwell, up and down, as the MIB wrenched her gun hand up and pinned it against the wall with his free hand. She felt the cold muzzle press savagely into her breastbone, and the P-38 fired once. The report was curtailed greatly by being pressed into her chest, and her heart was splattered like a water balloon inside her rib cage.

Her face registered more surprise than pain or shock. She sighed and her eyes fluttered.

The MIB let her go. Her body slid down the wall to the floor and shuddered once, then she was gone.

Her killer retrieved the athletic bag and examined the contents as the MIB guarding the basement door and Newport joined him on the first floor. Newport retrieved the silenced .22 and admired its lines.

The bagman whistled. "Jesus Christ! There's enough C-4 in here to blow this tower to the moon, sir!"

Newport checked the contents of the bag and nodded. "I think we have our shooter."

Lauren Hunter's killer sneered. "Yeah, and she isn't any Mack Bolan, either."

"All right, slick. You bagged her so clean up your mess. Take her body upstairs with the others and make sure she gets disposed of likewise."

"Yes, sir."

The MIB left the bomb bag with Newport, holstered his weapon and heaved Hunter's body across his back in a fireman's carry. He started the eleven-floor climb. Newport pointed to the basement door guard.

"You stay on this door now. If somebody comes up the stairs from the basement, kick them back down the stairs."

"Yes, sir."

Newport picked up the fallen beret and stuck it in the bomb bag. He headed back up to three to put a sense of urgency into that clean-up operation. They were taking too long.

MACK BOLAN HAD BEEN monitoring the enemy tac net with much interest. Joe Newport was a take-charge kind of guy. He had to give the man that much credit. He decided against venturing farther up the tower at this time. He was armed only with two hand-guns and several extra magazines for both weapons. It was something in his bones, some innate combat sense that told him it was time. No more fishing for the small fry. Time to bag the big fish. The recon was over. He had infiltrated the enemy, located the enemy and now it was time to smoke them.

He was going to need his duffel bag for that.

Bolan took the north stairwell back down to one. He stepped back into the busy atrium and headed for the registration desk, where he'd left Saracino.

His MIB gofer was still in front of the registration desk, with the duffel bag slung over his shoulder. A very nervous little dwarf of a man, balding with a thin mustache, was wringing his hands and involved in a tense exchange with Saracino. Bolan strolled up and took the duffel bag off his man's shoulder. Saracino spun with a start, then relaxed when he saw who it was.

"Oh. Great! I'm glad you're back. I've got you a room."

"Okay. Let's go."

He turned to head for the stairs but the hotel manager yelped, "But what about the emergency?"

Bolan spun on the guy and looked down at him menacingly.

"There isn't any. It was a false alarm, okay? Some kid with an M-80 cherry bomb or something."

"But I called the cops!" He pointed at Saracino. "He told me to!"

"Did you tell him to call the cops?"

"I told him to lock down the elevators, sir."

Bolan regarded the manager.

"So unlock the elevators and apologize for the inconvenience when the cops get here."

"But they might fine me, the hotel! You Feds are responsible for pulling this fiasco! I think you should deal with it!"

"You know what?"

"What?"

"I think you should sprout a couple of testicles. Come on, Herman."

Bolan turned and headed for the south stairwell doors. Saracino stayed right with him, shaking his head and chuckling.

"Damn, I like the way you operate, Mr. Donato."

"That's why they pay me the big bucks, Herman. What floor are we on?"

"Five. Room 505, sir."

"Okay, cut the sir shit, Herman. You're doing good by me. I appreciate it. Call me Tony."

"Yes, sir! I mean, Tony."

"That's better. These radios have more than one channel, don't they?"

Saracino nodded. "Yes. Three alternate channels with scrambler."

"Okay. You and I, we're on channel three now. Switch your radio, Herman."

Saracino reached inside his suit coat and switched the channel.

"What's going on?"

"Nothing yet. But I might need you for something special, and I don't want the rest of the world listening in on it, okay?"

"You've got it. Is there going to be real trouble? Do you still think Bolan's alive?"

"Yeah, there will definitely be some trouble." Bolan left it at that.

He pushed open the door to the stairwell. The landing was empty. He hit the stairs and took them two at a time. Saracino had to run to keep up. The third-floor landing was clean. Absolutely immaculate. No blood. No tissue. Nothing. Newport was a magician. He made those bodies disappear pretty damn fast. The sharp scent of pine solvent hung in the air. The landing was still damp from the mopping it had just received.

The Executioner bounded up the rest of the stairs to five and exited onto the floor without waiting for Saracino. He waited at the locked doorway of 505 for Saracino to catch up. The man pounded onto the floor a moment later, looking and sounding a little winded.

"You've got the damn key, I hope," Bolan growled.

"Sure," he breathed. "Right here."

Saracino produced a key card, which he stuck into the slot above the knob. There was a click and he twisted the knob, opening the door. He moved aside and let his superior go in first. Bolan stepped into the room and turned on the lights. He looked around briefly while Saracino came in and closed the door behind him.

Bolan put the duffel bag on the bed and went to work.

He took off his black suit coat and removed the double shoulder rig, which he laid on the bed, then he unzipped the duffel bag. Saracino just stood there watching, his eyes getting bigger and bigger as Bolan rigged for heavy combat. He pulled out the menacing SWA-12 shotgun, slapped in a magazine of buckshot, racked a round into the chamber, put the weapon on safe and handed it to Saracino.

"Here, Herman. Hold this."

Saracino was like a kid looking at a new toy. "Jesus Christ! What the hell is this?"

"The latest in assault autoshotgun technology. It's a prototype. Not too many of them like it in the world, at least not yet."

Next out was the black tactical assault vest, packed for bear with the full spectrum of rounds for the shotgun. There was a Ka-bar fighting knife on the vest, as well as several different flavors of antipersonnel ordnance. Bolan smoothed down his black silk tie and put the vest on over his shirt. He buckled the straps across the chest and cinched in the sides for a snug fit. Then he retrieved the double shoulder rig and put it back on over the assault vest. He pulled out a dozen extra magazines each for the Desert Eagle and the 93-R and stuffed them into free ammo pouches on the waist of the vest.

Finally, he pulled out a pair of black leather gloves with the fingertips cut off. He put on the gloves and flexed his fingers for a good fit. He zipped the duffel bag and put his arms through the two shoulder straps so that the bag could be carried on his back like a rucksack. Left inside the duffel was a two-hundred-foot rappel rope, a rappel seat and an assortment of snap links.

Bolan left the suit coat on the bed. He didn't need it anymore.

"All right. Give me the shotgun back, Herman."

Saracino handed the shotgun back to the Executioner. The guy was looking him up and down. Bolan cut an impressive and very intimidating sight.

"What do you need all that for, Tony?"

Bolan frowned at him. "Good God! Because Bolan's still out there, Herman! Wake up!"

Saracino just nodded.

Now Bolan was all business.

"Listen to me, Herman. I want you to stay here and listen to that radio. I don't want you to budge from this room unless I call for you, got it? I don't care what's going on. I don't care if you think the world is ending or if a 9.0 on the Richter scale should start shaking the hell out of the whole damn state of Texas. You stay here. Do you understand?"

"Sure, Tony. Anything you say."

"Good man. You're going to make it, Herman. Just do what I tell you to."

Saracino nodded again.

Bolan went to the door and opened it. He paused and said, "Hey, if I don't see you again, Herman, it's been fun."

And then he was gone.

7

Midland-Odessa Airport

Hal Brognola felt as if he were going behind his wife's back or something equally irrational. Bolan was going this one alone because it was personal. Hal Brognola had tagged along with an interagency task force loaded on four C-5 Galaxy heavy lifters for the same reason. It was personal. At times Stony Man Farm was his home, too. The people who were lost were his family, as well. And Brognola wasn't the kind of guy who liked to sit at home while somebody else scored all the points against the bad guys. He had to do more than just wait for word that the score had been evened, that the punishment had fit the crime. He had to contribute to this one. If for no other reason than to make sure that Striker had a safety net. Something to catch him if he fell.

The friendship went back too many years, too many miles. They'd started this strange ride on opposite sides of the law and, yeah, at one time Brognola had vowed to bring the outlaw Bolan in one way or another. Dead or alive because he was the lawman and Bolan was the bandit. That was then and this was now. Bolan didn't have to worry much about the lawmen anymore. In a strange extralegal way, the Executioner was a lawman now. He was the law of last resort. Jungle law turned against the jungle predators.

And here he was, chasing Bolan across the country again. Brognola wasn't in the chase to bring Bolan down, like in the old days. He was just making sure the guy made it home again, period. Because home and family were terrible things to lose.

Home and family, sure. That was what it all boiled down to. Everything Bolan did and believed and fought for could be distilled to those two words: home and family. The two things in life most sacred and the most worth living for and, even more so, worth dying for.

Brognola was torn from the depths of his own thoughts by the flight engineer saying, "We've got you patched through to Virginia, Mr. Brognola."

"Oh. Right."

He took the offered headset and put it on. "Brognola."

"Good evening, Hal," Kurtzman began. "I've got that satellite feed you wanted ready. I'm looking down on the target, and everything looks as peaceful as standing pond water. Jack's bird is just sitting there in the desert being wasted. There's nothing on infrared. No fires, no bombs going off, not even tracer trails. I can't believe Striker's down there. He must be somewhere else."

"He went in as one of them, Bear. He's probably

busy playing on their worst fears and setting them up to shoot it out with each other. He doesn't have to be bombing and shooting everyone in sight. Sometimes he just gets them to do the work for him.''

"Personally, after what happened here, I'd like to see a little fireworks.''

"Have you talked to Jack?''

"Yes. Right before I got through to you. He's wondering what's going on, as well. He dropped off Striker at the rendezvous point, and that's the last he's heard in about an hour.''

"That means something should be breaking loose very soon. I'm rolling. If anything changes, call me on the cell.''

"Roger.''

Brognola took off the headset and said, "Okay, let's get the noses up. We're going to be taking the convoy vehicles only. The three JetRangers will stay with the C-5.''

The captain nodded and relayed the word to the other planes. Brognola stood up from the navigator's position in the cockpit and hit the steep ladder down to the cargo deck. A loadmaster was at the controls next to the crew hatch activating the hydraulics that would lift the nose visor up and away and lower the load ramp.

The cargo deck was packed tight with twenty government sedans parked two abreast and ten deep. Two more of the C-5s were packed with the rest of the sedan fleet, fifty-six cars in all. The fourth C-5 was carrying the three Bell JetRanger helicopters from the U.S. Marshals Service.

Brognola yelled to be heard over the hydraulics at the loitering federal agents waiting for the word.

"Let's get ready to roll! We're going in! Sedans only! We're leaving the choppers on the bird!"

It was time to strike another blow in the good fight for home and family.

On the Tenth Floor

BOLAN DIDN'T ENCOUNTER any more MIBs on the trek up the stairwell to the tenth floor. All the better. He didn't want the shooting to start quite yet anyway. There was one thing he had to attend to first.

The eleventh and twelfth floors were already determined to be free-fire zones. Noncombatants, however, occupied the tenth floor. Bolan had to clear them all out first and create a buffer zone between the guilty and the innocent before the first shot was fired. When it came to noncombatants, Bolan didn't play fast and loose. He took innocent lives very seriously.

He exited the stairwell and started the round-up by banging on the first two doorways to his right and left. Bolan waited for a few heartbeats, then rapped on both doors again. The doorway on his left opened, and a pretty thirty-something woman peered around the door. She gasped at the sight of Bolan the war machine.

"Don't be alarmed, ma'am. I'm a federal agent. You and whoever else is in there with you needs to get off this floor immediately. You need to go down to the lobby and stay there.''

''What's going on?''

''There is a possible terrorist situation on eleven and twelve. That's all I can say. You need to go. Now.''

The door on the right side hadn't opened yet. Bolan assumed that the room was unoccupied at the moment. He went to the next two and repeated the process. The first woman he'd spoken to hurried out of her room with her overnight bag and purse and ran to the elevator. The doorway on the left again was the one that opened. The Executioner found himself looking down at a wide-eyed boy of about eight years old.

All the kid could say was *''Wow.''*

''Is your mother or father here, son?''

The kid shook his head.

''Are you alone up here?''

The kid shook his head.

''Who is here with you?''

''My sister.''

From inside the room, MTV was blaring loudly and a female voice yelled, ''Who's at the door, Jimmy?''

Jimmy turned and yelled back, ''A big man with lots of guns!''

''What?''

Bolan spoke up. ''Young lady, you and your brother need to go downstairs to the lobby right now!''

A pretty blond girl of about fourteen ventured toward the door, wearing a half shirt and cotton panties. Her eyes widened at the sight of Bolan.

"Young lady, get some clothes on and take your brother downstairs. This is not optional. You have to go. You're both in danger."

"Okay! Okay!" She ran back around the corner. A moment later she was in jeans and dragging Jimmy toward the elevator.

The kid couldn't keep his eyes off Bolan while waiting for the elevator. Bolan went down the line, pounding on the doorways. Most of the doors didn't answer. The occupants of the ones that did didn't waste any time in making a beeline for the stairwell or elevator once the occupants got one look at the Executioner in full combat regalia.

Once the Executioner was satisfied that ten was clear, he hit the stairs and went up.

TWO MIBS STOOD guard outside eleven. They hesitated when Bolan appeared on the landing below, armed to the teeth and looking like the harbinger of the Apocalypse.

The Executioner smiled and said, "Relax. I'm Donato."

That seemed to reassure the two somewhat. The guy on the right said, "Hey, Donato. You can stand down. We got the shooter. It was some bitch. Can you believe that?"

That was a curve ball Bolan hadn't expected. Some bitch? Bolan mounted the stairs, closing in.

"Then you got the wrong shooter," he said.

"What do you mean?"

"I'm still here."

The Executioner brought up the combat shotgun and let two thundering 12-gauge rounds sort it out for the two guards. The curtain of steel BBs shredded both men from the hips up, grinding flesh and muscle in blood sauce, and splattered the walls, ceiling and floor with gore like some new kind of grisly art form. An invisible fist swatted both of them backward and tacked them to the wall, but the two men didn't stick. Their bodies were crumpling to the floor as the Executioner bounded up onto the landing and wrenched open the door to the eleventh floor.

He bellowed into the open hall, "Hey! Hey, goddammit! That son of a bitch is shooting again! I need some help out here!"

Doorways up and down the hallway popped open, and a dozen of the black-suited SS shooters ran out of rooms with pistols drawn. A few of the guys had no faith anymore in their P-38s. These guys were packing Uzis and Bolan had to wonder at the irony of that: the modern-day descendents of Bormann and Hitler wielding burpers made by the Israelis.

Bolan dropped from view and went back down the stairs at a run, unhooking a fragmentation grenade from his vest. He pulled the pin and let the spoon fly as he jumped down the last five stairs to the landing below. He let the bomb cook off as the door up there banged open and the MIBs spilled onto the landing, opening fire without having a real target. The Executioner lobbed the grenade as the stairwell reverberated with booming single muzzle-blasts and full-auto fire. The OD green egg arced up into their airspace and went off like concentrated doom in the confined space right above their heads.

Bolan jumped into space as the ear-splitting detonation rocked the stairwell with a violent seismic tremor. He hit the landing on ten and slammed into the wall. Upstairs, the monstrous overhead concussion and red-hot shrapnel caved in skulls in that hardcore classroom demonstration of the power of physics, courtesy of the battlefield professor himself. The men standing in the doorway when the bomb went off were ejected down the hallway in smoking mangled heaps.

Bolan had kept his mouth open to equalize the air pressure in his head when the grenade went off, but his head was ringing violently. He wrenched open the door on ten and sprinted down the open hallway, going for the north stairwell door on the other side.

Now it was just a matter of staying ahead of them, hitting them from front, back and above faster than they could track on.

Move like lightning, sound like thunder.

The Executioner's campaign platform had always been about the politics of blitzing.

Mack Bolan was taking the fight right into their laps, up close and very personal.

JOE NEWPORT WAS in front of the elevator in the private alcove on the twelfth floor when the floor lurched violently and the muffled sound of the grenade going off somewhere below filled in the causal gaps. The crystal chandelier rocked on its moorings, and fine particles of dust fell from the ceiling onto the white marble of the entryway.

Newport stood talking with three of his SENSOPS agents, one of them Woods, when the balloon went up.

"What the hell was that?"

The door of the penthouse was yanked open, and Brent Dunphy rushed in, looking wild.

"What the fuck is going on, Newport? I thought you had this situation defused! Am I going to have to find somebody else to do this job of yours right?"

Newport ignored Dunphy while he barked over the command net, "Any station below! This is Newport! Report! What's going on down there!"

Somebody was still left alive down there to report in.

"Shots were fired in the stairwell! Somebody yelled for help, and then a grenade went off! I don't know how many are dead! At least six. Maybe more!"

"Who is this? How many men are still alive?"

"This is Mr. Seven, sir! I'm helping take care of the trash detail. I've got two guys with me. I don't know what's left in the other rooms."

"Well, find out!"

"Yes, sir."

Newport snapped his fingers at Woods. "Get down there, and take these two with you! Take the elevator and get some organization going with that guy! Move!''

Woods punched the call button, and the doors parted immediately. He and the other two MIBs piled into the car, and the doors closed.

"Get that air asset of yours on the roof right now, Newport!" Dunphy bellowed. "We're evacuating the Committee immediately!"

Newport turned to face the man. His eyes were aflame with a cold fire that had no more reason left to continue the ruse.

"We'll evacuate, Brent, when I'm fuckin' good and ready to evacuate. Now get back in there and—"

"You're not running this goddamn cell, Newport! I am! You do as I say or you're not just out, you're dead!"

Newport's hand was a blur of movement. Dunphy's eyes flared wide in wonder and hate, and he tried to beat the SENSOPS chief to the draw. But Newport was a stone-cold assassin. He had his P-38 unleathered and in the A cell commander's face before Dunphy could get his fingers wrapped around the butt of his own weapon. The P-38 exploded at a range of about one foot, and Dunphy's head snapped back grotesquely as the back of his skull erupted with blood and brains. The body catapulted back into the penthouse and crashed to the floor in view of the remaining members of the executive committee. Newport followed the corpse in and stood over it. He pointed the P-38 at the dead man's head and emptied the remaining rounds of his magazine. The rest of the skull flew to pieces, and when the bolt of Newport's weapon locked back on a smoking chamber, there wasn't much left of Brent Dunphy's head.

Newport dropped the magazine while keeping an eye on the rest of his associates.

"Anyone else want to tell me how to do my job?"

The remaining men of COMCON were too stunned to move or even argue. Newport fished a fresh magazine out of his suit coat and slid it into the butt of his weapon. He thumbed the slide release, and the bolt cycled a fresh round off the top and into the chamber.

"Good. Now the rest of you cool your heels in here and don't think about budging until I say differently."

Newport pivoted on his heel and stalked out of the penthouse, closing the door behind him.

THE EXECUTIONER BANGED into the north stairwell and bounded back up to the eleventh floor again, hitting the floor from the opposite side this time. He edged the door open and peered down the hallway to see what his opposition was doing. The hallway was in pandemonium. A dozen or more of the MIBs were out of their rooms, yelling in confusion and creeping up on the stairwell door on the other end of the hall. Another ten stood in doorways up and down the hall, waiting for the mob in the hall to reach some kind of a conclusion as to what was going to happen next.

Bolan helped them along with that analysis. He plucked another grenade off his vest, yanked out the pin and rolled the bomb down the hallway. The grenade bounced and careened. One of the guys gawking from his doorway caught the move in the corner of his eye.

"He's behind us!"

The MIB fired at Bolan with an Uzi as the soldier ducked back into the stairwell and crouched against the concrete wall. Two dozen 9 mm holes punched through the stairwell door, the bullets chewing the concrete on the far wall.

Somebody in the hallway yelled, "Grenade!"

The floorboards rumbled with frantic footwork and the walls thumped as the hallway mob went crazy, survival kicking in with the ugly ethic of every man for himself. The MIB tried to empty the hallway in the span of a heartbeat, and there just wasn't the time or the maneuvering room for everybody to take cover.

The grenade went off and the tower shook again, like the hand of God teasing the structure with total collapse. The bedlam of the explosion was quickly replaced with the cries of the maimed and the dying. Bolan reached out and grabbed the doorknob, throwing the door open. He leaned low around the jamb to assess the results of the grenade blast. The hallway had five casualties on the floor, two of them still hanging on to life by a thread. The rest of the MIBs had dived back into rooms or spilled into the stairwell at the other end of the hall.

Now every doorway down the hall was playing Jack in the Box as MIBs popped around the jamb long enough to point and shoot and take cover again. Three guys, one at a time, dived out of the elevator alcove and leaped across the hall and into the room on the other side. Bolan stuck the muzzle of the SWA-12 around the corner and triggered two explosive rounds. He was rewarded with another scream and a splash of blood that painted white walls red. He slung the shotgun over his shoulder and pulled another grenade off his vest.

He pulled the pin, counted down the numbers and tossed the bomb around the corner to the left and into the room closest to the stairwell. Somebody just had the time to yelp before the grenade redecorated the room with shrapnel, fire and flesh.

The stairwell door at the other end popped open and several Uzis opened fire, spraying the hallway with copper-jacketed slugs.

Bolan was concerned about the gunners in the other stairwell. If they thought about it, they'd see that dropping down to the tenth floor and running across to the north side would be a very savvy tactical move, forcing Bolan to divide his fire between two fronts. They might bring him down if that happened.

The Executioner needed some fire support. He keyed the mike to the tac radio on his assault vest.

"Mother Goose, Mother Goose, this is Striker, over."

JACK GRIMALDI ALREADY HAD the engines running. After talking to Kurtzman and giving his sitrep, he decided that he'd better be prepared to fly on a moment's notice. Bolan would be counting on him, and

Grimaldi knew that the time it took to do an engine startup could spell disaster for the hellfire soldier. The Stony Man pilot was ready for action when the call for fire came through.

"I'm here, buddy," Grimaldi responded immediately.

"Get in the air and swing around to the south side of the tower. I want you to put a rocket through the wall of the stairwell on the eleventh floor."

"Presto requesto," Grimaldi said, and took the black avenger into the dark west Texas night.

8

The rocket blew a hole through the concrete wall as big as a Buick. The fireball and debris was vomited across the eleventh-floor landing like dragon's breath, and the men crouched around the stairwell door ceased to exist in any form that would be recognizable as human flesh and bone. The violence of the blast enlarged the south side door and took down parts of the wall and ceiling of the two suites that were on that end of the floor. A tongue of fire mushroomed into the dark sky above the tower, and pieces of jagged concrete rained on the rooftop of the larger complex below.

Bolan stayed low, his body pressed against the concrete wall until the concussion wave stopped shaking the building like a tall tree in a strong wind. He didn't bother to take the time to eyeball the scene in there. Bolan wanted to keep them reeling and dying faster than they could regroup and counterattack.

He keyed the mike clipped to the collar of the assault vest. "All right, Jack. Swing around to the west side. Take out every room with the nose cannon."

"Roger that."

Bolan couldn't hear the gunship as it wheeled around the south of the tower to the west face and parked in the sky fifty yards off the line of balconies on the eleventh floor. There was no mistaking the sound of that Vulcan cannon cutting loose with hell-fire and brimstone. It was like a giant bull alligator roaring a challenge, something prehistoric and very hungry. The nose turret pivoted from south to north, hosing down the entire length of the tower at chest level. The explosive 20 mm shells gutted the rooms, making short work of the drywall and steel studs, obliterating the hallway. The turret corrected at the north and razed the floor again as the gun panned back to the south side. The eastern face of the eleventh floor vented the fires and wreckage of walls and shattered furniture in a cloud of combustion.

"Cease-fire!" Bolan yelled into the mike.

He waited for several breaths and listened. He didn't hear anything but the crackle of burning fires and the popping of live wires and severed electrical conduits. He pushed up to his feet and warily ventured onto the eleventh floor.

The floor was gutted, transformed into a bay of death and destruction. Bolan slung the shotgun across his back and pulled the 93-R free as he stalked the hellgrounds looking for survivors that needed a mercy round. Nothing. No survivors.

The elevator was relatively unscathed. A body was lying half in and half out of the car, and the doors were trying to close. The doors would slide toward each other, hit the body and open again. Bolan eyed the body and spotted the jagged shard of picture-window glass sticking up out of the guy's back like a translucent red shark's fin. This guy didn't need any more help getting deader than he already was.

The Executioner proceeded deeper into Hell.

Movement ahead and to his left attracted his attention. Bolan kicked through the remains of a wall, leading with his weapon. Somebody was trying to crawl out from under a collapsed wall. It was another of the enemy shooters. Bolan delivered a mercy round, ending the guy's misery. A strange odor permeated the atmosphere in that area, grinding out the stench that clung to the floor everywhere else. The smell was acidic and sulfurous; it burned the nostrils and watered the eyes. It was coming from the Jacuzzi whirlpool in what had once been the part of the floor plan devoted to the washroom. Chunks of drywall covered the big tub and obscured what was inside. Bolan pulled away a section of the debris and grimaced. A corpse was in there, one of the guys he'd shot on the third-floor landing shortly after arriving on the scene. The body was half-eaten away by acid, flesh, blood and bone bubbling away and leaking down the drain. On the floor next to the tub was something that froze his blood.

A shock of long blond hair jutted from under another pile of debris. Bolan attacked the broken gypsum board and threw it away with powerful heaves and shoves. Underneath the collapsed wall was the woman he knew only as Lauren Hunter. She didn't look too worse for the wear except for the bleeding hole in her chest where the bullet had cored her heart.

The MIB's words in the stairwell echoed in his brain: "We got the shooter. It was some bitch. Can you believe that?"

He stroked her hair and fought back against a wave of emotion. "You were a good soldier, Lauren. I only wish I knew your real name."

Bolan couldn't leave her there. It didn't seem right. She was dead, sure, but she was a soldier of the same side, and a good soldier never left a fallen comrade behind. It just wasn't done like that. The rest of the mission could be in jeopardy because of this, but he couldn't stand to think she'd end up a Jane Doe in a morgue somewhere.

It was unacceptable.

He might not have the time, but he was going to make the time.

Mack Bolan, the consummate soldier, went to work, knowing exactly what had to be done. He laid the combat shotgun on the floor next to Hunter's body and shrugged out of the arm straps of the duffel bag on his back. He unzipped the bag and pulled out the rappel rope, snap links, rappel seat and a sling rope that was five feet long. He took the sling rope and tied the ends together quickly with a square knot, then half hitched the ends of the rope on each side of the knot.

Next he stepped into and buckled the rappel seat around his waist, clicked a snap link into the ring in front and uncoiled the rappel rope. He tied off one end with an end-of-the-line bowline knot and wrapped the rope around a concrete support pylon, exposed now by the 20 mm firestorm Grimaldi's gunship had unleashed. He wrapped the rope tightly with three turns, clicked a snap link into the bowline loop and fed the running end of the rope through the gate of the snap link. He took the coil of unanchored rope to the balcony railing and threw it over the edge. The rope uncoiled in a straight, untangled line all the way to the rooftop nine floors below.

He moved over to the body and fashioned a buddy harness out of the ring he'd made with the sling rope. He twisted the rope to make two loops that looked like a butterfly. He lifted Hunter's torso off the ground and fed her arms through the two loops so that the X in the rope was in the center of her chest. He turned and sat down back to back with the corpse. There was more than enough rope left on the two crisscrossed loops for Bolan to get his arms through. He stood, and now Hunter's body was riding on his back like a human rucksack. He retrieved the combat shotgun and slung it over his head.

"Jack," he said over the radio, "meet me on the lower rooftop. I'm rappelling down now."

"I see you. Will cover."

Bolan clicked the rope through the gate of the snap link on his rappel seat, looped it around the solid shaft of the snap link, tested the strength of the anchor point, then climbed over the railing. He leaned back until his upper body formed an L with his legs braced against the edge of the balcony. He had his right hand behind him holding the running end of the rope against his buttocks as a brake. His left hand held the rope in front of him. He kicked off into space and threw his right arm straight out.

The rope whined, feeding through the snap link as Bolan and the dead woman plummeted through space on that narrow lifeline. His falling arc took him down four floors. Bolan braked as he swung back in toward the building. He flexed his knees and braced for impact against a balcony rail on the seventh floor. It was a short hop the rest of the way.

GABRIEL AQUARIUS HAD no intention of dying this night. He had narrowly escaped being blown into hamburger during the Executioner's raid on Tranquility Base back in early May. His survival instincts were finely honed. Everything in him was screaming to get the hell out. He wasn't going to wait on anyone to tell him when to run or where. Joe Newport had gone completely sideways, and Aquarius wasn't keen on placing his welfare in that lunatic's hands. Especially after seeing him execute Dunphy as if the man were some kind of rabid dog.

Bombs, fireballs and chain guns were lighting up the night and rocking the tower like a crowd in a heavy-metal concert. It was only a matter of time before all that action moved up one floor into the penthouse. Aquarius didn't want to be anywhere in the vicinity when that vulture came home to roost.

Aquarius was in the master-bedroom suite with his twenty-four mind-controlled girls, who were still dressed in their bikinis. He was opening weapons cases that had been brought up by several MIBs on Newport's orders. The cases were packed with Uzi submachine guns, ten to a crate. He stacked magazines and loaded all the weapons, twenty-five of them lined up in a row on the carpet in front of him. He needed one for himself.

He said to the girls in a steady monotone voice, "Girls, it is time now to call your operator. Code Alpha-3-Zulu. Follow the yellow brick road."

The change in their demeanor was spooky. They went from striking provocative poses to cagey feral killers in the twinkling of an eye. Their eyes iced over with malice and cruelty.

"Follow the yellow brick road," all of them replied in a chorus.

"That's very good, girls. My associates and I are leaving this place. You girls will stay here. Anybody who tries to enter this place after our departure is to be killed. Is that clear?"

"Kill the intruders," the teens chanted.

"Very good."

Aquarius handed each one of the young women an Uzi. Each took the weapon, racked the bolt back and held her weapon at the ready. He knew that when Bolan or whoever it was out there raising hell tried to take the penthouse, that person was in for a shock.

Aquarius moved out to the den and his troops followed. The eleven remaining members of the Committee were frantic, trying to track on what was happening from the windows and on the patio. They were all armed now, as well. William Laforge paced back and forth, ranting and waving his Uzi in the air for emphasis.

"That bastard! We should have killed him, not demoted him!"

Steven Reinhard burst into the room from the patio and yelled, "One of our helicopters is out there! It just blew the floor right under us out the other side of the building! What the hell is Newport up to?"

"I think we've been had," James Corr said calmly.

"Yeah, we've been had!" Laforge yelled. "That rat fuck! I'm going to kill him!"

"We need to think about getting out of here," Luther Gehlen said. "Newport can wait till later."

"I don't know about the rest of you," Aquarius stated, "but I'm going up on the roof. Newport's got a helicopter out there, and that's going to be the only way out."

Aquarius didn't wait for them to vote on it. He headed to the front door and took the private stairwell to the roof. The members of the Committee didn't wait to be invited. The eleven men hurried to follow him up.

9

"I was wondering when you assholes would get the balls to come up here," Joe Newport said, stepping out from behind an air-conditioning unit as big as a boxcar. He held his weapon down at his side.

Gabriel Aquarius and the eleven remaining members of the Committee were clustered on the tar-and-gravel roof before him, out in the open like ducks in a shooting gallery. Laforge went off like a powder keg.

"You've been up here hiding on the roof? You sorry sack of shit!"

Laforge wasn't a warrior. He was a desk jockey, an administrator. He telegraphed his intent like a neon sign. He jerked the Uzi to his shoulder, but Newport was already holding the P-38 at full extension, beating him to the trigger pull by a second. That was enough to determine who survived.

The Walther banged out one sharp report and drilled Laforge's throat. The man gurgled, clutching at the wound, then crumpled to the roof.

Nobody moved.

Newport laughed. "And then there were ten."

James Corr spoke up. "What are you doing, Joe? Have you lost your mind?"

"No, I lost my dignity. And now it's time for you assholes to pay the piper."

"Jack," Corr said, "you of all people should understand the system of rewards and punishments. You do the job right, you get rewarded. You fuck up, well, you pay a price. That's all that happened here."

"Oh, save your military bullshit for the Navy guys you send out to sea. *Nobody* does me like that. You hear? Nobody."

"Bolan's not dead, is he, Jack?" Gehlen said.

Newport snorted. "No, hell no. He's alive and well, and I invited him to this party tonight."

"I see."

"Yeah, those lights are finally coming on, aren't they? You poor dumb bastards."

Newport pulled a radio out of his jacket and keyed the transmit button.

"Mr. Kolchak, please bring my bird up to the roof. I need you up here now."

"Yes, sir. I'm coming in. ETA thirty seconds."

Gabriel Aquarius could see that he was stuck in the middle of something that he would have rather been excused from. He wasn't on the Committee. He just worked for these fascists. If not them, then somebody else. He was a merc. A businessman. His wares would always go to the highest bidder. Surely, Newport had no intention of bringing his hammer down on him, too.

"What's going to happen now, Mr. Newport?" Aquarius asked.

Newport looked annoyed, as if Aquarius didn't have the proper credentials to be talking to him, let alone asking questions of him.

"Aquarius, you're not part of this. Why don't you go stand in the corner or something? This is between us men."

Aquarius carefully backed away from the group, keeping his eyes on Newport and his gun hand. He went to the edge of the roof and stayed there, cradling the Uzi. He waited to see what the outcome of this sad story was going to be.

"Are you going to kill us, Joe?" Oscar Batt asked.

"I thought that that was the perfectly obvious intent to all of this, dumb fuck."

Batt, Gehlen and Corr were the fighters in this group. They knew how to kill and had a lot of training with firearms as part of their respective backgrounds. Especially Batt and Gehlen. Gehlen made the first move. He rolled across the roof, angling to the left away from the group, and fired on Newport from a prone position. Batt and Corr both went into action, jogging to the right, firing on the move. The others just gawked in brain lock before getting into the action, as well.

Newport had anticipated that they'd try to kill him first. It was only natural, especially among these feral dogs. He ducked back behind the giant air-conditioning unit and ran. He heard several pairs of feet grinding gravel across the roof, pursuing him. It would be the three hunters. The other Committee members were firing blindly, stitching holes across the metal housing of the air-conditioning unit. They were clueless, as dangerous to one another as they were potentially to Newport. He dodged out from behind the air conditioner and ran down between a line of big ventilating units. An Uzi chattered from the rear, and sparks flew off the metal housing close enough to make him duck.

Newport spun and fired back.

It was Gehlen behind him, closing like a shark on prey.

Newport dived between two ventilating units and sprinted to the other side. Where was Kolchak and that helicopter? Bush Wainwright and Steven Reinhard were running toward him as he popped out from in between the ventilation units, and they both fired from the hip. The bullets weren't even close. Newport skidded and pivoted in their direction, dropping to a crouch as he did so.

He picked them both off easily with two skull shots. And then there were eight.

Newport dived away from the open space between the ventilation units, sensing rather than seeing Gehlen pop into that narrow corridor. Hot 9 mm rounds chewed up the roofing where he'd been crouched a second before. He ran farther south. He was going to run out of roof soon.

He wondered where Bolan was. This was supposed to be his gig.

BOLAN SHRUGGED out of the buddy carry rig on the lower rooftop as Jack Grimaldi brought the Stony Man AeroDeth in to skim the deck. Bolan transferred Lauren Hunter's body to his shoulder and ran to the crew hatch on the chopper. He threw the door aside and placed the woman's body on the deck, then jumped inside. He pulled her by the shoulders to the rear of the troop compartment and left her there. He keyed the mike as he moved back to the open hatch. He readied the SWA-12 for action, dropping the magazine and replacing it with a fresh one.

"Take me back up to the roof, Jack."

"Roger."

The superstealth chopper lifted off in a dead vertical climb straight back to the top of the tower. Bolan felt his stomach drop into his boots, and strained to stay in a crouch. The G-force of the climb wanted to press him into the deck.

The helicopter slid sideways at altitude and was over the rooftop. Bolan had the combat shotgun in hand and jumped into space, hitting the rooftop and rolling as four or five subguns opened fire on him, probing for his range. The gunners were poor shots. None of the bullet strikes came near him. The rounds were flying from two different directions, and Bolan had to make a snap decision as to which direction would find his range first.

He came out of his roll and dived onto his belly on the rough gravel surface. He had two choices in targets—the gaggle to his left or the lone gunman near the edge of the roof toward his two o'clock. The gaggle was obviously inept. The lone gunman was doing it right. He had an Uzi, and after firing his first quick burst at Bolan and missing, the guy went low and took the time to unfold the stock on the weapon.

The Executioner triggered two rounds into his two-o'clock position.

The range was about twenty-five yards and the steel-shot pattern had spread into a curtain of death. The guy's upper body became a splash of flying blood and tissue. He was punched off his feet and tossed over the edge of the roof. Bolan rolled to his right, correcting as he did so.

The gaggle was five-men strong, but these guys were dilettantes when it came to using a firearm. They also didn't seem to understand the concept of spreading out in a firefight. They were staying in a tight group as if the closeness gave them strength. Their proximity to one another might make them feel good about themselves, but it did nothing to improve the survival odds.

The Executioner burned them down easily. It was like a turkey shoot.

He stood and walked toward his vanquished enemies. The five men were laid out like stiffs in a game of sudden-death Twister. He studied the faces, recognizing Henry Klinger and Mason Jefferson, undersecretary of state and banker extraordinaire, respectively. The other three men Bolan wasn't familiar with, but he memorized their faces twisted in the rictus of death so he could ID them later.

The sound of three Uzis rattling off wildly to the

south put Bolan on the defensive immediately. The shotgun was up and probing for a valid target. The huge block structure of the rooftop air-conditioning unit to his front obscured everything that was going on south of him. There was a terrific noise, and a plume of fire and smoke erupted over the top of the giant unit. With the fireball's climb into the sky, a black helicopter rose up, its nose cannon speaking again.

Two men raced from between ventilation units downrange, skidding around the corner on leather-soled shoes. They had nowhere to go. Bolan recognized both men: Oscar Batt of the FBI and Admiral James Corr of the Joint Chiefs of Staff. Before Bolan could engage the two traitors, the helicopter did an aerial pirouette and the Vulcan cannon saved Bolan the ammunition.

Ten yards of flame erupted from the rotating barrels of the cannon, and the two men disappeared off the rooftop. There'd be no miracles of reconstruction for the funeral done on those two. Bolan doubted that there was even a teaspoon full of biological material left between the two of them.

The pilot caught sight of the Executioner on the rooftop, and the chopper dipped and made a strafing run on Bolan.

The Executioner might as well have been unarmed.

NEWPORT HAD RUN OUT of roof.

He skidded to the edge just as the black chopper lofted into view. The pilot raised the helicopter high enough to get the rotors clear of the edge of the building and rocked the bird in sideways until about three feet of open chasm remained between the lip and the open crew door of the AeroDeth. Uzis were yapping behind him, and he leaped across the space and crashed onto the deck, sliding into the opposite bulkhead. He was on his feet immediately and taking a seat at the CIC. He plugged in his headset so he could talk to the pilot and activated the nose cameras.

He had twenty troops on board. The storm troopers were buckled into their web seats and deep in the theta dream state. He had no reason to bring them around to beta. The bird pivoted in midair, and Newport found himself looking down the length of the rooftop, toward the north, via the monitor in front of him. He saw Gehlen bolt out from between the ventilation units. The look on the man's face when he saw the hovering AeroDeth was priceless. Newport switched on the recorders so he could have a tape of this to entertain himself with when there was nothing better on TV.

"Blast that fucking rat," he ordered the pilot.

The pilot did a rapid eye switch, and the cannon roared in a short two-second burst. Gehlen was blown to bits. The sight made Newport giddy with warm feelings. He loved removing mental midgets from the face of the earth. It was such a rewarding calling in life.

He saw Corr and Batt skid into view farther down the line. Those two knew a lost cause when they saw one. Both ducked back between the ventilation units and ran. Newport had no idea where those two thought they were going to go.

"Pursue and eliminate those two dopes."

The helicopter lifted and shifted up and over the ventilation units. The two runners were already on the other side, on a relay race to nowhere. The gun spoke again, and that run became a fire walk into nonexistence.

And there *he* was, downrange, standing over the bodies of the remaining Committee members. The Committee was dead, and now there was only Bolan left to kill. The other AeroDeth that hovered on the north end of the rooftop was certainly a concern. Newport was a betting man. He bet that his flyboy could smoke the Executioner before Bolan's flyboy could do anything about it.

"That's Bolan," he said. "Blow that bastard up."

GRIMALDI'S CHOPPER CHARGED, going straight at Newport's bird on a certain collision course. The Stony Man pilot gave no indication that he had any intention of pulling up or veering off. The other guy was going to have to do that or the two helicopters would try to occupy the same space-time coordinates, which was still a physical impossibility.

Grimaldi had a talent for playing chicken.

The other pilot pulled up at the last possible second and barely cleared Grimaldi's rotors. The enemy bird cleared the rooftop on the north end and banked sharply to come back around for a second try at Bolan. The Executioner didn't stand around to see if

Grimaldi was going to interdict the guy again. He raced for the edge of the roof on the east side, looking over the lip for some place to jump to. The balcony of the penthouse jutted out beyond the lip of the roof dozens of feet below, to the south.

Bolan backed up, then took off like a jaguar on speed.

Grimaldi swung his bird around; the tail traded places with the nose at the north end of the roof and the Vulcan cannon drew a line in the sky, daring the other bird to cross it. The enemy helicopter twisted in the air and showed Grimaldi its flank, and the high-tech polymer armor absorbed the 20 mm burst with ease. Then the pilot of the enemy bird pivoted back on target and fired two rockets.

Grimaldi had to abandon station, diving wildly to the right in a roll that dropped the chopper below the level of the roof as the two rockets flew through the space just vacated and kept on going into the night.

That tactic was deliberate. It gave the other pilot the opening he needed to make a second run at Bolan.

The Executioner was at the jump-off point. He went over the edge of the roof, his feet pedaling beneath him as he dropped and the Vulcan roared behind him. He hit the deck and rolled as that section of roof above him blew apart in fiery chunks, debris raining across the balcony and patio in sizzling chunks. The black shadow of the helicopter flew over the lip of the roofline and dropped to spin around. Through the picture windows, Bolan saw sections of the ceiling fall to the floor and pin several slight figures underneath.

Bolan heard rockets fire and he reckoned that this was it, that he'd finally met his death.

He was wrong about that. The rockets had come from Grimaldi's chopper, flying back onto station low on the north side. The two air-to-air missiles flew up at the enemy, who had to break and run or get blown out of the sky. Grimaldi's helicopter rose up over the railing and hung there in space, standing guard over Mack Bolan.

Over the tac net, Grimaldi reported in. "Looks like they've lost their stomach for it. They're breaking off and heading west."

Bolan detected movement to his right on the other side of those floor-to-ceiling windows, just a flash of bright colors, but it was enough to signal danger and he hit the deck as fifteen Uzis ripped loose and peppered the area Bolan had just vacated. The glass exploded and sparks flew along the flank of the hovering gunship where the bullets impacted instead. The gunship swung around to return fire with the nose cannon.

Bolan got a look at his opponents, and his eyes widened.

"Jack! No! They're just kids!"

10

The Executioner could have had it worse. The enemy pilot could have missed the lip of the roof with cannon fire meant for him, and Bolan would have more of the little wiry killers to worry about. He could see the sprawled and unconscious bodies lying on the carpet and under chunks of the ceiling, Uzis sitting on the floor where they had been dropped. As it was, his hands were full with fifteen adversaries. He had no doubt that they'd all keep trying to kill him until he put their lights out. The young women were all very pretty and very unnerving in their skimpy bikinis and stiletto heels, brandishing Uzis like pros as they advanced through the shattered picture windows with murder in their young eyes.

None of them could have been much older than sixteen. Bolan had a good idea of what these girls had been put through and why they were there. Fodder for old degenerate men with monstrous needs and appetites. And if sex was no longer exciting enough, they could be transformed into stone-cold killers with a snap of the fingers and turned loose on a defenseless public.

But if it came down to him or them, could he kill them? And if he did kill one or more of the young women, would he be able to live with himself afterward? Was staying alive and living to fight another day more important than their young lives? All he could think was that these girls were somebody's daughters.

Bolan wasn't going to shoot back no matter what happened. That was a blood vow made right on the spot. His crusade wasn't worth that. If these girls killed him here today, so be it.

He needed some combat stretch.

The soldier sprinted to the left, behind a concrete pillar, and the girls tracked him with fire blazing from the little Israeli submachine guns. The bullet strikes chewed furrows in the concrete, and ricochets whined in the night. Bolan used the butt of the shotgun to smash the window in front of him to make an entrance into the penthouse. The young killers were flanking around the patio, focused on the pillar he'd ducked behind, and Bolan had a clear stretch right across the huge den to the hallway that led to bedrooms.

The black helicopter sluiced into the airspace directly over the patio, and Grimaldi hammered the young assassins with a violent hurricane wind produced by the rotor wash. The girls' hair was lashed and sucked up overhead, and the gale-force wind swayed the featherweight killers like reeds. Three of them stumbled and fell. Two hit the flagstone with enough force to be knocked senseless, which seemed to give Grimaldi an idea. He started smacking the girls down with light nudges from the landing skids. He knocked four more senseless while the others retreated and opened fire on the helicopter.

Now there were nine left, which was slightly better than having fifteen to contend with.

Bolan ran across the den, down and through the sunken level and back up the other side. He made the hallway and ducked around the corner as the nine girls caught his scent again. They charged back through the ruined window frame with the Uzis rattling away on full-auto.

The Executioner knew that he just had to get them to use all the ammo in their magazines and they'd be his. He didn't see any extra magazines stashed away anywhere on those nonexistent swimsuits they wore.

He checked the first two bedrooms, which were empty. The last room was the master suite, and he hit the jackpot. Several open weapons cases were laid out in there along with the extra ammo. He definitely had to deny this piece of terrain to the girls.

Bolan hurried through the doorway and slammed it behind him. He locked the door and stayed well to the left of it. He had a strong sense of how the girls would deal with the locked door.

He was exactly right on the money.

The wood paneling began to fly apart as the nine girls emptied the remaining ammo in their Uzis through the locked door. Bolan knew they were out of ammo when they began to attack the weakened door with kicks and buttstocks.

Grimaldi's voice came over the tac net. "Hey, Sarge. I think Hal just drove up with the cavalry. Should I have him send some marshals up to save you? Are those girls kicking your ass?"

Bolan just growled. He didn't have time to dignify smart remarks like that with a comment.

A delicate foot inside a stiletto heeled shoe crashed through the door panel. The girl left the shoe on Bolan's side of the door when she pulled her foot out. Bolan pulled a flash-bang grenade off his vest. He'd let them get through the door and drop the senses mangler right in their midst.

Bolan took up a position in the bathroom, leaning around the corner and watching the door being chopped to pieces with bare hands, feet and buttstocks. When the door finally gave up the ghost, it split right down the middle and the half with the knob fell onto the carpet while the other half swung into the bedroom on the hinges.

The Executioner pulled the pin and tossed the stun bomb into the mob.

He ducked around the corner and went low, closing his eyes and covering his ears. The bomb went off with a blinding flash and earsplitting noise. Every window in the room blew out into the night. Bolan heard the girls toppling over and thumping against walls like bowling pins, and ventured back into the bedroom.

The girls were no matches for the stun grenade. They were out cold.

Now he had to subdue them while they were down

and out. He pulled the Ka-bar fighting knife out of its sheath, produced a fifty-foot length of parachute cord from a pocket on the vest and began to cut up sections two feet long. He tied the girls' forearms together behind their backs, then went into the den and tied up the girls knocked senseless by the ceiling collapse. Finally he emerged onto the flagstone patio again and tied up the last six.

He got on the SENSOPS tac net and said, "Hey, Herman. Get your ass up to the penthouse. I've got a job for you."

SARACINO HAD BEEN sorely tempted to budge from the room on the fifth floor throughout the terrific battle that was raging above. He spent his time running back and forth from the window to the open door, where he'd look up and down the hallway for anyone coming from the stairwells. He didn't see anybody exit from the stairwells the whole time the war was being waged. But he saw the whole fifth floor bolt from their rooms and scramble through the stairwell doors to get the hell out of Dodge.

When Donato hailed him from the penthouse, he honestly hadn't expected to hear from the guy again.

"Yeah, Tony! I'm here! Jesus! What's been going on? Was that Bolan raising all that hell? Did you get him?"

"Yeah, Bolan's up here. Come on up and see."

"What kind of job you got? A shit detail?"

"No, it's not a shit detail. Mercy detail, let's say."

"What?"

"Just come up to the penthouse. You'll see when you get here. Take the stairs to the eleventh floor, then take the elevator from there."

"Shouldn't I just take the elevator from here?"

"There's a body jamming the door up here. So it's stuck on eleven. Get the picture?"

"Oh. Sure. I understand. I'm coming up."

"Make it quick, kid. My numbers are gone."

Saracino ran out of the room and hit the stairwell, nearly setting a record for covering six stories. He was in the south stairwell, and when he got to ten he could see the hole in the outside wall where the rocket had detonated.

"Jesus Christ," he breathed. He went all the way up to eleven, and the condition of that floor was absolutely frightening. He'd never seen such destruction in all his life. He found the elevator, and sure enough there was Shark Fin lying there. He dragged the body out of the way by the ankles and got on the car.

A nagging suspicion had been chewing away at the back of his mind for some time now. He didn't want to believe it because he really did like Tony—or whoever he was. He wondered what he was going to do about it if his suspicion turned out to be true. He better be prepared. He pulled the P-38 out of the shoulder holster and clicked off the safety. And he realized then that he was trembling.

If he was right, he had every reason to be trembling.

Saracino punched the number 12, and the doors

closed on him. The elevator car felt like his own private mausoleum.

THE EXECUTIONER SENSED that Saracino wasn't an idiot. The guy was going to put two and two together soon. Bolan just hoped that he wasn't stupid. He fed a fresh magazine into the Desert Eagle and waited for Saracino to enter the penthouse.

Shortly thereafter, Bolan heard the elevator door open. Light footsteps pattered across the tile, then the front door opened with a creak.

"Tony?"

"In here, Herman."

The MIB entered the den slowly. He looked around the place, at Bolan, the girls tied up on the floor and finally at the body of Number 12 lying at his feet just inside the den. He looked at the mess for a long moment.

When he looked up, Bolan could see that the guy had made all the necessary connections. He could also see that the guy was trembling, his knees almost knocking together.

"Did you do this, Tony?"

Bolan shook his head. "No. I think Joe Newport did."

"Are they all dead?"

"Everyone but Newport. And you."

Saracino nodded and checked out the room again, as if he might have missed something visually important in his first scan of the surroundings.

"You've got your gun out, Herman," Bolan said.

Saracino looked at the pistol as if he were still deciding what to do with it. Bolan could tell the MIB really didn't want to go there.

"Uh-huh. I see you have a gun out, too."

"I don't have to use it, Herman."

Saracino made eye contact with Bolan's frosty blues and held the gaze. He didn't flinch. The guy might be a little unsure of himself, a little green, but he had grit. It was moments like these that men showed themselves for what they were deep down in the heart.

"You said Bolan was up here. Where is he?"

Bolan let a heartbeat, then two pass.

"I think you know the answer to that question."

Saracino studied his shoes. It was true, then. He was right. Still, the P-38 stayed at his side. It felt as if it weighed a hundred pounds. He couldn't find the will to bring the piece up. He knew he'd be dead before he could even get a decent sight picture.

"It's over, isn't it?"

Bolan nodded. "Almost. It'll be over once Newport is dead."

"It would be stupid of me to stay on a sinking ship."

"That ship already sank, Herman."

"Yeah, I guess it did. I'm going to put my gun away, okay?"

"Okay, Herman. I'm happy you decided to play it like this."

Saracino made double sure to keep his trigger finger completely away from the trigger as he slowly opened his coat and slid the weapon back into his shoulder holster. Bolan watched him very carefully as he did it. As soon as Saracino's weapon was stashed, the Executioner holstered the big silver .44 Magnum pistol.

"So, ah, what's my assignment, ah, Tony?"

Bolan smiled. Playing it smart all the way.

"There are twenty-four young ladies here that need to get down to safety. They're tied up more for your own safety than theirs. I'm not exactly sure how to turn them off, if you know what I mean."

Saracino nodded. "Yeah, I know what they are."

"Okay, then. Well, I'm curious, Herman. What's the phrase that pays?"

"What? To turn them off?"

"Exactly."

"Once upon a time in America."

"That's the phrase?"

Saracino nodded. "And touch them on the knee. The left knee."

"Herman, that's too easy. You should have seen what I went through to get them like this."

"I'm wondering something myself, Tony. Why didn't you just kill them?"

"I don't kill innocents, Herman. These girls didn't ask to be made into robots without a will."

Saracino nodded and thought about that. After a moment's reflection, his face was split by a broad grin.

"I like the way you do things, Tony."

"So, can you handle the mission I'm giving you?"

Saracino nodded enthusiastically. "I can handle it fine."

"There's a Fed in the parking lot named Hal Brognola. Seek him out when you get down there. Tell him I sent you. He'll take care of you."

"Yes, sir. And what about you?"

"I've still got one more guy to bag before I call it a day."

"Well, you get that son of a bitch. I never liked him."

"That guy's one of a kind."

Saracino walked forward and stopped an arm's length away from the Executioner and stuck out his hand. Bolan took the other man's hand and the two of them shook on it.

"It's been a pleasure watching you work, Tony. Good luck."

"It's been a pleasure watching you turn over a new leaf, Herman. Don't let it go sour again."

The Executioner turned and exited onto the patio. Grimaldi's AeroDeth helicopter was still hovering off the railing, standing guard like a faithful dog. It was orientated so that Bolan was seeing the side of the bird with no troop door in it. He made circles in the air with his index finger.

The black helicopter stayed in the same place in the sky but rotated around the axis of the rotor shaft. Grimaldi raised the bird slightly and nudged over to the railing. Bolan hopped up on the railing and jumped into the stealth chopper. He closed the troop door behind him and told Grimaldi to land in the parking lot. Bolan wanted to have a parley with Brognola.

The AeroDeth swung away from the building and dropped altitude.

HAL BROGNOLA HAD TAKEN his sedan out of the parking lot and continued north toward Amarillo after the message from Grimaldi came over the Stony Man tac net. He pulled into a secluded rest area and got out of the car. He walked into the flat desert a hundred yards to the east. The black AeroDeth helicopter was sitting quietly in the darkness, invisible from the rest area and prying eyes. Mack Bolan stood outside the chopper waiting for his arrival.

"Mission accomplished, Striker?"

Bolan shook his head. "One more fish to fry. Newport is still at large."

"Okay. But the other thing—it's dead, right?"

"Yeah. As dead as it's going to get. What are you doing out here?"

"I need to get out of the office once in a while."

"Yeah, but fifty-six cars, Hal?"

"And three JetRangers."

"Oh? I guess I missed those."

"They're still on the C-5."

"I need you to take charge of a package for me, then we have to scoot. Newport's got a head start."

"Okay. What's the package?"

"Come on."

Bolan led the big Fed onto the black helicopter and took him to the rear of the troop compartment. Brognola wasn't expecting to see a body waiting for him back there.

"Jesus, Striker. What's this?"

"A good soldier, Hal. I couldn't leave her behind."

"Who is she?"

"That's what I'd like to know. I only knew her as Lauren Hunter."

Brognola closed his eyes for a moment, saddened by yet another loss of a soldier on the same side.

"Well, let's get her in my car."

Bolan shouldered the burden of carrying the body off the helicopter and across the dark landscape. He had her cradled in his arms and he placed her gently in the backseat of Brognola's car.

"Thanks, Hal. There's a man in black back at the travel plaza who's turning over a new leaf. He's doing a favor for me. I told him to escort some innocents to the parking lot. Don't be too tough on him, okay?"

"You've got it. Where are you headed now?"

"Bear is tracking Newport from orbit. We're going where he's going."

Brognola nodded. "Okay. I'm going to be following your progress, as well."

"What? You're going to be following me again?"

"Hey, I have to get out of the office sometime."

The two old friends shook hands, then Bolan turned and disappeared into the darkness.

11

Nevada

The mysterious base was located inside 4,724 square miles of restricted airspace called Dreamland. Groom Lake in southern Nevada was one of many dry lake-beds scattered through the desert all the way into California and Death Valley. Located in the wide Emigrant Valley nestled between the Timpahute and Pahranagat mountain ranges, Groom Lake was inside the Nevada Test Site, which was part of the four million acres of bomb ranges that made up the Nellis Air Force Base Bomb and Gunnery Range. In all, a chunk of real estate bigger than Belgium.

The perimeter of the base at Groom Lake was bracketed with hunter-orange fencing with the same message plaque hanging every twenty-five yards: U.S. Government Facility. Deadly Force Is Authorized. Photography, Drawing And Sketching Is Prohibited. Twenty yards inside the fence were funny silver balls, the size of basketballs, mounted on top of poles fifteen feet high, with one silver ball every fifty yards all the way around the base and the airfield. The airfield was a single runway, seven miles long.

Looking down from atop Freedom Ridge or the Whitesides Mountain, the base seemed nondescript and unimportant to the naked eye. Lines of unimaginative buildings and barracks, and a row of huge hangars lined the parking apron adjacent to the runway, fuel tanks, a big radar dish and almost no foot traffic on the "streets" night or day. Speculation on this fact inevitably led to the conclusion that the buildings were interlinked by underground walkways.

The Wackenham crew—camouflaged M-16-packing private soldiers contracted to provide physical security for the base—constantly patrolled the perimeter. The security force wore woodland-camouflage fatigues in the desert and looked as if they'd been trained by Gold's Gym, not Delta Force. They had a reputation for wildly unnecessary aggressiveness. With their mirrored shades, boonie hats and tie-down special-ops holsters, the security detail oozed testosterone and menace.

The base was unique in that it was officially under the command umbrella of the Air Force but run *for* the Air Force entirely by civilian defense contractors. Everybody had a different name for the place. To the black aviation boys of the Skunk Works, the base was called "the remote location" or "the Ranch." Air Force pilots out of Nellis called the Dreamland airspace "the Box" or "Red Square."

The name for the base that had become hard currency in popular culture was Area 51.

Area 51 was like an accounting mirage to most branches of the federal government outside a small clique inside intelligence and Air Force R&D. Freedom of Information Act and media inquiries into the existence and purpose of the secret facility at Groom Lake were met with unanimous denials right across the board—"Area 51, to the knowledge of this agency, does not exist."

For a place that didn't exist, the track record for creating and fielding strange "Buck Rogers" aircraft was even more remarkable. The U-2 spy plane had emerged into service via Groom Lake. The SR-71 Blackbird rolled out of one of those Air Force hangars that could be seen from the tops of Freedom Ridge and the Whitesides Mountain, as had the F-117 stealth fighters. Darker rumors persisted about the base. According to UFOers, Area 51 was in possession of captured extraterrestrial technology that was being subjected to concentrated attempts to "reverse engineer" that technology and apply it to Air Force projects. Rumor intelligence—RUMINT—suggested that the reverse engineering was only now yielding workable technology.

The base at Groom Lake was home to some of the biggest names in the military-industrial complex of the cold war era. TelBech, eSystems, TWR, Hues Aircraft, AICS, Heed-Lockengruven Aerospace, GG&E and, of course, Global Investigations and Executive Security, LLC.

The base switchboard operator had a list of building numbers and extension numbers inside each building. That was it. Which contractors occupied which buildings and the names of the individuals at each building's extension numbers was strictly limited and controlled information. Phone operators had no need to know. Callers asked only for building numbers and extension.

Building 23 was leased out entirely by the federal government, and FEMA was the agency's name representing the Feds on the leasing document. The agent at extension 23 had a base directory that listed all the names and whom the paychecks were being cut by. The agent was always dressed in black and worked for SENSOPS, the secret heart that beat inside the FEMA facade.

The unseen hand with the all-seeing eye that ran everything that did or didn't happen inside the security fences of the Groom Lake facility belonged to COMCON. That information was classified fifty-six levels higher than top secret: MAJIC clearance was required to pry open that folder and only to those with a genuine need-to-know.

At the South Gate

THE WORST THING a Groom Lake employee could be was late. Late happened sometimes. Most employers understood this. However, the federal government was a very different breed of employer inside the Dreamland airspace. It was considered very stupid to miss the Garnet Airlines flight out of Vegas every morning direct to the remote location and having to drive to work. Being severely AWOL from the job was the least of the obstacles on the gauntlet facing the stray unfortunate who drove up and idled in front of the first gate at the south entrance.

Heather Richards had been thirteen minutes late in arriving at the airfield, and the plane wouldn't return again for almost twelve hours. Twice a day, seven days a week, the 727 shuttle planes touched down and taxied onto an apron that was located at the opposite end of the property from the Las Vegas International terminal. She'd driven to the airfield anyway in the hope that someone there might call ahead to let somebody know that she had been left behind.

There was no one at the airfield.

It took her a little over an hour to drive in from the airport.

Richards had been driving on a dark dirt road with the surreal orange fence line paralleling each side of the road for what seemed like a mile before the South Gate came into sight. She didn't know that her civil rights had been consensually surrendered where the dirt road suddenly transitioned to a fence-protected corridor that funneled her into the dead end in front of the first gate.

A video camera digitally encoded her profile. She fished her ID card out of her purse and rolled down the window. She fed the card into a reader slot on a box console with a ten-digit keypad, then typed in her seven-digit PIN.

The red light on the console stayed constant while the computer checked its records.

The red light winked to green, the reader spit out her card and Richards returned it to her purse. She settled back in her seat and expected the first gate to roll open.

Instead a speaker mounted in the video camera raven-perched to the card-reading console barked orders to her in a gravelly male voice.

"When the gate opens, Ms. Richards, you will drive your vehicle into the containment area, turn off the engine and get out of the car. Is that clear?"

The rough voice startled her; she jumped.

"Oh! Um, yes. Okay! I'll cooperate fully! I missed my flight this morning. Is there somebody you could call?"

"We've informed the proper people," was all the voice would offer.

With a loud metallic clanging as gears came to life, the chain-link gate mounted with battleship plate lumbered back slowly on wheels that squeaked. The containment area was a large rectangle of asphalt, the guard shack being the middle point. The shack looked more like a concrete bunker with two-inch-thick glass windows on three sides.

Four white men, blond with crew cuts and absurdly overdeveloped bodies, stood in the high-beam glare of Richards's 1993 Chevy Chevette like stone pylons. All of them wore the same mirrored lenses and carnivore smiles that reeked of violation and trespass.

Richards braked and shut off the engine. She left the key in the ignition as the biggest of the blond supermen stepped up to the driver's side of the car. The vainglorious portion of golden scrambled eggs on the bill of his black SWAT cap IDed the guy as the probable man in charge.

The black-clad man-mountain was carrying a clipboard that looked like a matchbook in his hands.

He looked down on her, and she saw twin images of herself in the mirrored lenses. Richards didn't like the way she looked. She looked vulnerable and utterly alone. That carnivore leer tightened with more tension.

"Ms. Richards. I'm waiting."

The woman blinked. She really was getting nervous now.

"Ms. Richards. Were you not told to get out of the car after turning the engine off?"

"Oh! Yes, of course."

"Then do it, please."

The other three were moving around the rear of the car as she stepped out of it quickly. She closed the door behind her, put her hands behind her back and tried not to visibly tremble.

The big leader backed off ten or so feet.

"Step away from the car."

She stepped toward him. The three henchmen were behind her now, one each at her three, six and nine positions. Three o'clock and nine o'clock each held M-16 rifles at the ready.

"Ms. Richards, are you aware that there are certain penalties incurred when you break a vital pattern of behavior suddenly, like missing your flight in this morning?"

Richards was too scared to speak. She couldn't get her mind wrapped around the idea that being late for work was this dire.

"You have to look at it from where we are standing. We don't know if you have actually overslept or if you missed the flight deliberately by reason of subversive intent. We don't know which one you are. Which one are you, Ms. Richards?"

She tried to jump ahead in the exchange and see where he might be going with this. The sound of more than one helicopter flying in the distance scrambled her reception.

Her mind shuffled through vowel sounds.

"Uh, is there a problem?"

"That is what needs to be determined. Place your hands over your head, palms together."

She hesitated.

"That wasn't a request."

She slowly weaved her hands above her head, palms together.

For a man who was almost as wide as he was tall, she hadn't expected him to be able to move inside her space as quickly as he did. The clipboard clattered on the ground next to them and her blouse was torn open in a hail of buttons, both his massive hands fumbling over her breasts.

She was stunned by what this beast was doing to her.

The crack of her slap across his face was like a thick limb snapping in a violent wind. Her eyes were smoldering with anger and humiliation.

"I have rights—" she began in a full-steam fury.

The crack of the rifle butt was delivered to the back of her knee with a lot of sadistic strength. The cruel blow caught her off guard, the force of it propelling her onto both knees painfully. She had bitten her lip and tasted coppery hot fluids.

"You haven't got shit, bitch," said a flinty voice directly behind her, above her.

She was yanked to her feet.

"You surrendered all rights the minute you entered the Dreamland, Ms. Richards. Merely driving through the first gate grants consent to be searched to any degree deemed necessary in order to assess a subject's threat level. This must be thorough."

His hands yanked the nylon cups up off her breasts. Her wrists were seized and forced behind her. She felt the cold steel bands ratcheting down on her wrists, heard the cuffs locking down. She closed her eyes and tried to keep from crying.

He was minutely examining the material of her bra, feeling it for microphones or built-in miniature cameras. Then his hands were kneading both of her breasts, rudely and then her nipples were being rolled painfully between index fingers and thumbs.

After a minute of savoring the smell of the woman's fear, he stepped back.

"My men are relatively new to this industry," he explained. "They're getting valuable training in body searches this morning."

Cold water sieved through her intestines.

"Make sure I didn't miss anything," he told his men.

Three sets of hungry hands attacked her breasts, her bra, tummy, hair, face and mouth. Her breasts were aching with pain when he swatted them off after several minutes. Then his hands were on her again, spinning her and propelling her against the side of her car. His body pressed into her, crushing her against the car, then he hiked up her skirt roughly and twisted into the waistband. His fingers were between the elastic bands of her hose and her panties. He was sticking to the search scenario.

"Stay down against the car and don't try to turn around."

Richards froze, bracing herself. She knew it might not be over for a long time. They'd probably drag her into the bunker and take turns raping her for the rest of the day.

The pilot of the big white Bell JetRanger helicopter did an expert job of masking his approach vector. In the flash-fire heat of the moment, in a place where the sound of helicopters coming and going was a very frequent occurrence, the four gatekeepers were much more engrossed in Richards's defenseless state, bent chest down over the hood of her car. They were all caught in the million-candlepower glare of the search beam with both hands on their buckles.

To Richards, the voice that boomed from above riding on the righteous whirlwinds of divine intervention would always be more like God's in her memory. The voice belonged to Marshal Vince Pierce of the U.S. Marshals Service, and the helicopter was branded with the U.S. Marshals star on both sides of the fuselage.

"Put your hands in the air and back away from the woman! This is the U.S. Marshals Service, and by order of the President, you are all under arrest!"

That amplified authoritarian voice ricocheted around inside the containment area.

The doors were off on both sides of the helicopter, a marshal suspended in each door dressed in storm-trooper black, safety strapped into the chopper and each brandishing an identical SW-3 magazine-fed 7.62 mm NATO sniper rifle mounted with Starlight scope. The wash off the rotors was brutal.

The SWAT cap with the scrambled-egg bill was blown off the blond man's head in the artificial gale-force winds.

"You don't have the clearance!" he roared.

He yanked the Parkerized black Desert Eagle .50-caliber handgun clear of leather and tracked skyward. Three sharp reports and strobe-globe muzzle-flashes erupted in the open door of the hovering chopper, and the probable man in charge died instantly as the hydrostatic shock front of the three rounds blew his chest into black cherry puree.

The man-mountain fell over like a scale Godzilla. The other three looked at their dead but fearless leader doing the final nerve spasms on his back, and their weapons clattered to the pavement like hot potatoes.

A rope spilled out of the helicopter on the far side, and five agents deployed to the ground on Swiss seats. They hit the ground and moved to cover an open sector, leaning into the buttstocks of their suppressed MP-5s and scanning for evidence of hostility over sight blades.

The marshal in charge barked orders. "Secure the area! Let's get these gates open! Main body arrival less than one!"

Figure forty-five seconds to make it all happen. The biggest thing was getting the gates open. Marshals one and two stormed the bunker and seized the abandoned gate controls without incident. Marshals three and four used the stocks of their weapons to smash the remaining security guards to the ground and double flex-cuffed their wrists behind their backs with almost indestructible polymer bands. Methamphetamines or not, these brutes wouldn't be breaking free of their restraints without outside help.

The men were dragged out of the way by their collars. A marshal helped Richards away from her car and had a buddy search one of the guards until the man produced handcuff keys.

Richards was freed and she lowered her skirt, taking refuge in the bunker.

"Let's get this car out of the way. Get those gates open!"

A marshal dropped behind the wheel of the Chevette as the gates came to life and rolled away. He cranked over the ignition and drove the little economy car out of the way, leaving it behind the guard shack.

A charging convoy of white government-tagged sedans and panel vans was booming down the dirt road toward the first gate, running lights out, the drivers using military NVGs to stay out of the weeds. Two more Bell JetRangers were flying low in escort. Dozens of vehicles were involved in this multiagency and jurisdictional task force composed of agents from the Justice Department, the Marshals Service, FBI and the ATF. It was a Justice Department operation all the way. The locals had been left out of the net completely for reasons of operation security.

And the Fed leading this charge was Harold Brognola.

A reaction force of dozens of base security vehicles burned up the road from the direction of the base, chaffing to make contact with the intruders.

One of the marshals bolted to the edge of the open second gate and yelled his spot report. "Incoming! Enemy vehicles approaching from the north, maybe two dozen with more joining the charge!"

The marshal in charge yelled, "Let's cover that hole! Let's let the cavalry get in here!"

Every operative in this raid was issued the same tactical Motorola MX300 radio with crypto and VOX headset. The spot report had gone out over the net to everybody involved.

Brognola's voice from the lead car bearing down on the containment area likewise went out to all stations.

"The time for shy is over. They know we're here. All units, let's go live. Lights, sirens, high beams, spots—whatever you've got. Don't slow down. Drive right through the bastards. This is Justice One."

12

Inside Restricted Airspace, Groom Lake Research Facility, Nevada

Mack Bolan applied lead to the upper-left field of the target overlay, anticipating the target to dart there next.

The target went down.

Bolan's eyes were already up and to the right. The Vulcan cannon growled, fully committing a deadly cone of fire to a part of the sky where the target wasn't.

The Executioner corrected, dropping his chin almost imperceptibly to the right, raking the 20 mm electric cannon fire in a blazing slash across the tail of the target bird. Bolan's target was armored beyond the Pentagon's wildest imaginings, agile, and armed as well as the Stony Man bird was. The gunships were exactly identical.

But this time it happened. Something weakened in that unbelievable polymer armor both of the birds were equipped with. Flames billowed out behind the tail boom briefly before vaporizing into a smoky comet tail that glowed purple-white in the silver moonlight.

This chase had been going on forever. Nine hours now, nine hours longer than eternity.

The skill of the other pilot was beyond question at this point. This guy was everything Jack Grimaldi was. The guy had to be. He couldn't have kept this chase going as long as he had if he wasn't. Out of Texas, across two whole states and into Nevada. Unbelievable.

The skies above the whole world were within reach to a couple of combat aces flying two nuclear-powered helicopter gunships. Each was flying for keeps, trying to find the right combination that tripped up the other one.

Because in this game, there could be only one left to overfly the end of the line.

Bolan was up front in the chase bird, in the copilot-gunner's seat. All weapons controls were at his disposal. Grimaldi concentrated solely on staying with the quarry. Bolan's job was to bring the black bird down for good.

Joe Newport had thus far managed to remain in the sky, staying just beyond reach or putting obstacles in Bolan's line of fire.

The black gunship wallowing in Bolan's gunsights had to be blown out of the sky. The soldier couldn't call this over until the man on that sci-fi battle bird was dead. The Executioner fired a salvo.

The sight of flame issuing from the tail of the gunship ahead of them was like tasting first blood. Bolan had to continue to concentrate fire in that wounded area. The pilot would immediately begin maneuvers to deny Bolan that opportunity.

The Executioner kept the red LCD crosshairs over the smoking hole in the armor as the enemy pilot flew directly at the mountain looming in the flight path of both aircraft. Bolan kept firing and didn't worry about Grimaldi following the enemy into the dirt.

The enemy AeroDeth chopper jerked out of the collision course at the last possible second, rising up and over the sunbaked rock peak and out of the line of fire.

Bolan's eyes moved and the cannon fire terminated abruptly.

Grimaldi was anticipating the maneuver and easily mimicked the other pilot's stick and pedal work.

"He's not going anywhere, Sarge," the Stony Man pilot said over the VOX.

Bolan readied his weapons systems to reacquire the target as soon as the gunship popped out over the top of the mountain.

The sharp, high-G bank up and out of the collision corridor tripped an alarm inside the cockpit. Bolan's eyes were scanning through the sky for the quarry. He spotted the sinister dark shape lofting into the clear night air.

The fleeing helicopter was climbing into an aerial anomaly, something Bolan never expected to see. "Mother of God," Grimaldi said.

The ground was connected to the sky by a column made up of hundreds of luminous balls of...-

something. Bolan couldn't see through the objects, suggesting that the spheres were solid objects and not clever holographic projections. The objects were like round Christmas baubles with lightning halos. The lightning orbs glowed disturbingly, giving off a light that was produced by knowledge men had no business tampering with. The weird light of the orbs was a steady visual throb of differing colors: red, green, blue, violet and a daze-inducing bright yellow.

There was a weird hum in the air of the cockpit. The "sound" wasn't really auditory at all. It was at a lower level than that, a vibration that was felt in every cell, in every molecule of matter within proximity to the strange aerial phenomenon that the Stony Man warriors were flying toward.

The rainbow-colored lightning orbs lazily spiraled upward into an ever narrowing funnel and disappeared into thin air a thousand feet above the muffled rotor blades of the Stony Man chopper. The enemy aircraft seemed to be flying right into the part of the sky that the big Christmas balls were melting into.

Grimaldi had no intention of taking the stealth helicopter into the spiraling orbs. He was correcting course to put the AeroDeth into an orbit around the column of lights, this Jacob's ladder into the sky. Bolan locked the nose cannon onto the fleeing enemy chopper and opened fire.

A violent brush stroke of flame connected the distance like pyrotechnic magnetism. Rose blossoms of combustion popped all over the rear fuselage and boom, marking the impact of armored rounds with plumes of fire, smoke and debris.

The running helicopter continued the full-power ascent without even attempting to avoid the lethal hailstorm Bolan was feeding up the tailpipe. Somehow, if the enemy gunship intersected with that nexus the Christmas lights were disappearing into, it meant escape.

The Executioner couldn't allow that.

Somebody else wasn't going to stand for it, either.

Bolan wasn't sure what happened first: was it the blinding flash that bleached away the image of the enemy AeroDeth momentarily, completely wiped the helicopter from the visual spectrum, or was it the sudden disappearance of a frightening chunk of the sky?

The events had probably occurred simultaneously.

Bolan's cannonade of fire abruptly stopped.

The blinding flash was too bright and too fast to track back to a point of origin, a visual whiteout that occupied a sliver of time.

Bolan blinked. He focused on the part of the sky where the running stealth helicopter had eroded into the light. The helicopter wasn't there anymore. But there was something above now that had stolen a horrifying percentage of the visual airspace through the glass of the cockpit.

Grimaldi yelled over the com link, "Jesus! We've got a bogie! And it's huge!"

Bolan could see that. And all he could do in that moment was look, his head cranked back looking up through the Plexiglas at the unthinkable floating in the airspace above the whirling blades. The shape was hovering motionlessly above the Groom Lake facility a thousand feet higher than Bolan's gunship. The stealth helicopter was flying directly beneath the behemoth, and the soldier had to shift his gaze to his far left and right just to see the sky again.

The thing was shaped like a monster-sized delta that was made out of pure darkness, a black matter that gave off no light, no reflection. There was no sense of form or mass, just a huge spearhead chopped into the sky that looked like a hole into nothing. It couldn't be a solid object, a ship of some kind.

That was the naked eye's report.

Grimaldi's radar screen was reporting on the material reality of the thing overhead, but Bolan's eyes still told him that nothing was there—that the black delta was composed of a literal absence of everything. It was like a portal between two places that they could fly through.

Whatever it was, the thing was occupying a massive swatch out of the night sky. The delta ship was at least a half mile long, and was just floating there as if the effects of gravity were optional.

Dead center in the triangular blackness was a rectangle of reddish-purple light, and the lightning orbs were flying into the opening and disappearing into the interior spaces beyond.

Into some kind of cargo bay.

Whatever was at work here, as impossible as it all appeared, Bolan knew that it had nothing to do with magic. Science was at work here—science made into technology.

Grimaldi wasn't taking any chances about that flash of man-made lightning. The stealth helicopter dropped its nose and swooped toward the earth, trying to lose altitude as fast as possible. The abrupt reorientation of the chopper was just in time to catch the sight of the other stealth chopper just a second before splattering into the desert on a fall from the sky that rolled in widdershins spirals right up to the impact.

The impact wasn't a fiery production, more of a smoky flying apart of the airframe and tail boom as the aircraft burned into the earth with utter finality.

No survivors there, Bolan thought.

Now it was just a question of their survival.

It was a race to get to the ground before the weird weapon spoke again.

The helicopter was dropping like a stone through a power dive, but the light couldn't be outrun.

That white light came again, hotter this time because their helicopter was now the target of the beam.

It was a wave upon wave of screaming physical dissonance that didn't even last a second, but it was long enough to do the ugly work.

The stealth helicopter was coming apart, literally peeling apart as if every fastener and rivet had suddenly shrunk or ceased to exist.

Bolan clutched the arms of his seat, hoping that the cockpit kaleidoscope would remain a solid frame when the aircraft hit the dirt. It was a crazy bedlam of sight and sound and, before the blackness, lanced through with ice slivers of raw fear.

Mack Bolan didn't remember the actual moment of impact.

JOE NEWPORT DIVED for the deck, underneath the tactical console as several of the 20 mm rounds pierced the aft bulkhead and banged around the interior like sledgehammer heads doing the speed of sound. He was as flat as a man could be up against the deck plates; anything more and he'd begin fusing into the metal.

Something hot and wet drenched most of his back and the seat of his pants. Newport swallowed his gag reflex, knowing what had just happened—one or two of the soldiers packed into the belly of the aircraft had been blown to pieces by the ricocheting chunks of steel.

The 20 mm rounds were armor piercing and supersonic. The hydrostatic shock front on a round that big was fiendish. Tissue was turned into soup, and bone was blown into shards. A human being was transformed into big bleeding pieces of flesh that flew away from the point of impact.

It was ugly.

Newport couldn't afford to open his eyes and look.

A look might change everything right now. Looking to see the outcome of an event affected the very outcome of the event. Ask any quantum physicist.

Newport let it ride.

But it had been a bad bet all along. The man had

enormous talents that could be used in the service of good or ill, and he'd chosen to pedal his wares in stone-cold Evil's black company. He'd been doomed to this moment from day one, from the first day he crossed the line and began to work toward the end of civilization. Joe Newport had been penciled into the cosmic ledgers and was given a date to face Judgment on the day he stepped over the fence line and joined Evil in its pasture.

That day had arrived.

Newport saw the light through closed eyelids. It was light on a scale that penetrated all matter and pierced thought. For Newport, the light wasn't connected to his religious sense in any way. He knew that God Almighty wasn't swallowing their bird whole in the blaze of His glory.

It was simpler than that. But simpler didn't make the truth any less painful.

The *Graf Zeppelin VI* was firing on them.

The delta ship was a secret R&D refinement to the airship. The "disappearing" trick that the airship performed wasn't magic or actual physical transparency. It depended on extrapolations and refinements on technologies like video and liquid crystal display— LCD. Minute pinhole video eyes covered the hull of the ship. The surface of the hull was, in effect, one gigantic LCD screen on which the picture feeds from the cameras were displayed. What the video feed "saw" from the upper hull was displayed on the lower hull; likewise, the digital picture information captured by the eyes in the lower hull were displayed on the upper hull. The trick worked better at night. During the day, a good eye could see a minute difference and incongruency in cloud patterns and shades of blue that could give away the presence of the delta ship. She only flew at night.

The AeroDeth helicopter was seized in time and space completely for a fraction of a second. Everything came to a dead stop, everything except the force of the chopper's forward momentum at the time the beam caught them and held them tight for a split second. It was the force of momentum tearing through and away from the mass of the chopper that shredded the aircraft like a paper document in a wind tunnel.

Then the beam winked out, darkness and the stomach-churning sense of free fall filling the vacuum.

Newport didn't like his death. It had come way too soon.

BERNIE FOGELMAN was hoping to get lucky this night. He was alone with her. Finally. Just the two of them. The desert was too cold for the fair weather diehards inside MOFO, a cultlike splinter of a splinter of a UFO group that was spying on Area 51. Nobody knew what MOFO stood for. It was probably a word that had been painted on the bottom of a UFO, as AFFA had been.

Experts were still trying to figure out that sighting.

Fogelman couldn't think about UFOs right now or weird government aircraft reverse engineered from UFOs. The thought of what Beth Fletcher's nipples looked like in the starlight was at the forefront of his thoughts tonight.

He hoped that she had the same curiosity towards him. It would make things go easier.

But the light show ruined all chances of romance.

Fogelman lost it, shouting at the sky, "Who writes your material, man? I mean, you're burnin' the Bern!"

Beth Fletcher, a petite underdeveloped blond woman with big tortoiseshell horn-rimmed glasses and a hint of an overbite, was grabbing for the video equipment when Fogelman went off on God's inappropriate timing. The strangeness of his words wasn't lost on her. She aimed the camera at her companion and turned on the built-in light.

"Are...*they*...communicating with you, Bernie?"

The man's psychological boxcar derailed.

"What?"

"Is somebody other than you in communication with you?"

"I think God is trying to ruin my chances of getting laid!"

"Could *they* just be pretending to be God in your mind? What if they're trying to trick you?"

"What? Who the hell are *they* anyway? What did you take before coming out here?"

Fletcher gestured over her shoulder and clucked.

"Ah, hello. Bernie. Do you see those lights? Whoever is driving the lights is also the voice in your head claiming to be God. And you'd never have a chance with me anyway, so don't even think about it, you fiend.''

All Fogelman could do was blink. Fletcher filmed that dead-guppy look a few seconds more, then turned the camera back to the light show.

"I guess that *they* aren't communicating with you after all.''

Fogelman's fingers curled into fists. Before he could think of a suitable retort, something with a voice like an exploding volcano began to tear physical hell out of the mountainside to his rear. It was a sound right out of the Apocalypse that seemed to swamp the world in its noise. It was all so unexpected, and Fogelman was terrified of sudden detonations. His scream was shrill and girlish as he dropped to the ground on folded knees. A hurricane whirlwind suddenly put the atmosphere in a blender, a loud double whoosh as two huge black prehistoric shapes one after the other cannonballed over the peak and into the open sky. Fogelman didn't see any of this; he heard and felt the passing of the two unidentified flying objects barnstorming the mountaintop.

The heavy machine-gun fire startled Fletcher but her reaction was nowhere near Fogelman's panic level. She had a video camera in her hand, a one-chip Panasonic VHS-C with nothing very special about it except that it was old. In terms of where video cameras were right now, this box was from the dinosaur days of electronic evolution, back when vacuum tubes ruled the earth.

She spun in a fluid arc. The camera was on her

shoulder; her one-eyed gaze was through the view-finder. She was quick enough to catch the passing of the trailing object as it shot over the top of the mountain. She came back around and tried to get a good shot of one of the black things.

Fletcher had an impression of something monstrous and insectoid. She'd reviewed reports that, if true, had to lead to only one conclusion: UFOs might sometimes be alive. She quickly dismissed the possibility that these objects were biologicals. Even mutant biologicals wouldn't come equipped with heavy machine guns.

The night was almost sterile the air was so clear. Visibility was excellent with a half moon high in the sky. The UFOs were helicopters of some kind. Weirder than all hell. And so quiet. The two black helicopters corrected courses and soared up toward the vanishing point in the sky where the Christmas lights were blinking out of existence.

Fletcher began to comment on the scene the best that she could.

"The base you see below is the famous military secret code named Area 51. The beautiful colored balls taking off from the base are beyond words. This tape recording is probably the biggest event ever in the history of UFOs."

The chain gun boomed again, and Fletcher raised the camera skyward, framing the two warring helicopters.

"We've just been flown over by these two weird whirlybirds. They look like they're painted black, they're both real quiet and it looks like one is running from the other.''

Her verbal fount was momentarily dry.

That changed instantly when the black delta ship rippled through the star field and solidified two thousand feet above the Groom Lake research facility.

She had time only to yell ''Oh, Lord! What is that?'' Then came the white flash that bleached out the world for one hot second. The camera recovered from the whiteout quickly; the running helicopter plummeted earthward in a sickening, out-of-control spin. The helicopter was losing mass at a frightening rate. It didn't make it to the ground to officially ''crash.'' There wasn't enough left to still call it a helicopter: it was a rain of parts and human bodies, as if every fastener, rivet, bolt and pin had suddenly disappeared and the aircraft just fell apart.

The trailing helicopter dived almost immediately, following the bright flash in a mad run to burn off altitude before the inevitable. The aircraft was seized midway down, stripped of cohesion and released to rain across the bleak landscape of southern Nevada. Fletcher tracked the demise of the second helicopter. This one was caught and wrecked much closer to the ground. The pilot managed to bring the helicopter down with most of the mass intact with a belly flop that rolled through the bone-dry dust of the long dead lake bottom.

The Christmas lights lofted back into the belly of the mothership. The half-mile-long airship pivoted toward the south, toward Las Vegas and beyond the garish neon glare—toward the Southern Hemisphere. Fletcher videotaped the ship as it glided across the valley in the light of the half moon. Then the ship did that shimmer-melt into the star field and was gone again.

A press conference had to be called. Fletcher's highest priority right now was getting this tape back into the hands of the faithful before it could fall into government hands. Delta Force–trained security troops were more than likely converging on the mountaintop. They probably had very little time left.

She hated to leave Fogelman behind, but he was still in shock and would slow her. Without a backward glance she set off, picking her way through the darkness and loose rock quickly but carefully.

The Flight Line

"OUT OF THE FRYING PAN into the fire," Jack Grimaldi groused.

The captured AeroDeth was a piece of junk. Grimaldi had managed to keep the nose level and brought the chopper in for a belly-flop landing. As the dust settled, the helicopter continued to fall apart rivet by rivet. It wouldn't be long before the Stony Man specialists would be standing in a pile of parts inside a bare steel skeleton. That beam was devastating, whatever it was.

Mack Bolan was unbuckling, preparing to abandon ship. He let the flight helmet drop to the deck and retrieved his weapon, which was stashed below the seat.

The Executioner clicked off the safety on the SWA-12 combat shotgun. "Let's head out, Jack. We run for the gates and hijack something on the way that'll get us out fast. If it shoots at us, we shoot back."

"I love traveling with you. We fly. We crash. We run for our lives."

"Yeah, and that's the beauty of it. We don't run away from them. We run right through them."

Grimaldi pulled the Ingram MAC-10 .45ACP machine pistol from the custom leather rig he wore over his flight suit. He yanked back on the charging knob located on top of the weapon. The bolt locked back, open.

"Kind of like football, with bullets."

"Exactly."

Bolan booted out the small-arms-resistant Plexiglas pane on the flank and followed it out, dropping on top of it, then on to the white, hard alkaline soil of the dead lake bottom.

The Executioner was on the ground in Area 51.

Freedom Ridge

THE LIGHT SHOW in the sky was over, and Bernie Fogelman had regained his composure. What kind of weird irony was playing out on that dead lakebed below?

He was familiar with the lie of the land here. He

was a pro when it came to spying from atop Freedom Ridge. He knew every road, gate and intersection into the place and he knew every building, tower and suspected supply depot. The buildings were brilliant examples of blandness, of how a structure could be deliberately designed not to betray the nature of the work done inside. The buildings of the base were completely sterile: no numbers, no signs out front listing officers in charge, unit or organization names. There were rows of khaki brick admin buildings with mirrored glass, and dozens of huge hangars along the flight line. Beyond that were manufacturing shops and warehouses. Same colors, same anonymity.

The MOFO membership had a hand-drawn map of the base and marked the buildings that constantly drew their interest for one reason or another. Then they bet on which defense contractor was leasing the building being watched, the nature of the work being done inside the building being watched and the best ways to figure out whose speculations were right.

The security force seemed to radiate from that hub, so the smart money had already concluded that Building 23 had something to do with base security. They were right. But of all the guesses ranging from the CIA or the DIA as to whom was actually leasing the building, none of the gambling eye-spies thought FEMA might be the right answer.

Building 23 had a vast underground garage. The down ramp went below the alkali flats on the south side of the four-story admin structure. The exit ramp was on the north side of the building. A staggering number of security hardmen worked on the base. Wackenham Global was the number-one employer at Groom Lake. Every employee of every contractor operating inside Dreamland airspace had to work within eyeshot of a security guard. They had guards in the latrines. The females were watched on remote video feed and taped.

And all these guards had to have a vehicle to ferry themselves around in, back and forth between their shift assignments and central command. Foot traffic was a big no-no. Satellites could see people on the ground, well enough to digitally capture moles and names on nametags. Walking around on base was an offense that carried zero tolerance.

Fogelman kicked something in the dark that sounded hollow and made of plastic. He bent and pulled out the extra video camera, flicked off the lens cap and switched on the camera. Just in time.

What seemed to be an invasion of federal vehicles screamed down the road. The lead set of high beams and flashers let two from behind take point, as the security force's road blockage became a problem. Those two cars played chicken with the two leading the security team's charge. Neither side backed off or eased off on the accelerators. It was an impact that Fogelman could clearly hear from about a five-mile distance. Four vehicles collided. The invading Feds surged around the wrecks into the desert on both sides of the road. The security force to the rear of the collision didn't have the same playbook. They were reacting with locked-up ABS pads, their cars losing control and executing corkscrewing spinouts into the dirt and one another.

And then the shooting started.

Fogelman had maximum zoom applied, but the battle was still just bouncing lights punctuated by winking globes of small-arms fire. He couldn't tell who was shooting at whom. He could see the weapons rattling off from all sides in the tangled traffic. Three helicopters swarmed above the firefight and greatly assisted the combatants in shooting one another with wildly panning million-candlepower search beams. The distance washed out the sound of amplified voices over the gunfire.

He thought he could make out a few words like "marshals" and "arrest" and "surrender immediately!" The words were apparently falling on deaf ears. The only acceptable terms of surrender this night would be a bullet in the brainpan. The invading Feds didn't have any trouble dishing it up to the opposition on their own terms.

About ten of the Feds' vehicles stayed behind to pin down the Jeeps that had been sent to intercept. The rest of the federal force yielded to either side of the shooting war and were back on Q Clearance Boulevard once clear of the crash zone.

Security vehicles surged out of the underground lot on both sides of Building 23 and cordoned off the area, setting up hasty rings of defense.

And on the airfield another short-lived gun battle erupted. The muzzle-flashes appeared to be on the flight line itself on one of the bridges connecting the runway to the parking ramp. This whole scene had started out *Close Encounters* and was now somewhere closer to *Starship Troopers*.

But in the end, the civilian security force was defeated.

They were no match for the law.

On the Ramp

THE EXECUTIONER WAS armed only with what he'd departed west Texas with—the Desert Eagle, the Beretta 93-R and the SWA-12. He had on a black load-bearing vest that was packed down with magazine pouches for all three weapons, with the emphasis on keeping the shotgun well fed.

The two Stony Man warriors were running hard and fast across the runway tarmac, heading for the row of giant maintenance hangars that bordered the flight line for almost a mile. The landing lights were off, and the hangars were dark inside and out. The illumination from the moon was about thirty-three percent, good enough to see that the other guy was coming at you in night shades of gray and shadow.

The two soldiers saw the reflected beams of the headlights bounce out from between the sixth and seventh hangar in the row in advance of the vehicle coming into view.

"Think they're coming to give us a lift?" Grimaldi asked.

"No, but I think they're giving us the proper tool for the job."

The white Jeep shot out from between the hangars and wagged back and forth across the parking ramp like a wild beast correcting on the scent. The driver spotted the two dark figures silhouetted at the edge of the ramp and arced the Jeep around, bearing down on them. The man riding shotgun leaned out his window with an AR-15 rifle and fired, trying to find the range.

The Executioner went to one knee and sent that guy back range data encapsulated inside a 12-gauge deer slug. The AR-15 boomeranged out of fingers cut off from central control, and the guy caromed back inside the car, flopping into his comrade.

The driver stomped on the brakes in a panic. The SUV bore down on its nose and the tail sluiced, spinning the vehicle.

Bolan corrected to bring the driver's-side windshield under fire. Grimaldi beat him there, stitching a nasty oval in the glass, concentrating a baker's dozen from chin to breastbone. The driver let go of the steering wheel and his life in a flesh confetti effervescence. Flailing feet running on final nerve firings kicked the accelerator and brake sporadically. The Jeep jerked forward in lurches until the nerve firings burned out forever. The SUV continued forward at a crawl of its own accord.

Bolan ran forward and jerked open the driver's-side door. He threw the two corpses out and ran around the rear of the vehicle, yelling, "You're still the driver on this mission, Jack!"

He had been so wrapped up in the act of shoring

up their survival odds that he was only now becoming aware of the sounds of gunfire, lots of it, in the distance to the south.

Maybe it was the cavalry, although he knew that he had none on order. But there was no ignoring the fact that the enemy was fighting someone to the south. Bolan figured that was the direction they needed to go.

Pronto.

13

Q Clearance Boulevard

The sound of raw power growling in the acceleration curve filled Hal Brognola with a swelling sense of security. Women found security in bank cards and diamonds by the carat. Men found security behind the wheel of an extremely overpowered automobile. It was always important to a man to have the ability to drive around very fast if necessary.

The streetlights on the base zoomed into view, as did the blocky silhouettes of buildings and towers. The buildings were all dark, all of them in view. Streetlights and security lights were the only other illumination on the ground. Q Clearance Boulevard rolled through the center of the base like a main drag. Up ahead, a cordon of resistance came to life as headlights and flashers winked on in a barrier from one side of the street to the other, and a half dozen little red dots did a light show on the windshield in front of the head Fed's face.

Brognola dived beneath the dash as the windshield lost cohesion, dissolving in a fusillade of full-metal-jacketed rounds. The big Fed kept control of the wheel and did a job on the brakes. The white Caprice executed a slide that showed the ambush the broadside of the heavy cruiser.

The Justice man heard the three JetRangers roar in low over the top of the Caprice and the car was shaken righteously in the thunderstorm. The door snipers were ladling on viciously accurate return fire from above and bought the big Fed some breathing time. Brognola's abrupt stop had marked the line that the Feds were now going to stand on and advance from.

Caprices, Crown Victorias and panel vans were skidding off the road and over sidewalks, into parking lots and open desert to the right and left of the perpendicular command vehicle. Agents in trench coats, suit coats, shirt and tie and raider gear locked on to target from behind open doors and over roofs and hoods. The raiders had laser targeting gear, as well.

Red sabers of light crisscrossed the no-man's land between the two lines before the muzzle-flashes began to wink at one another with deadly accuracy.

Windshields and body panels on both sides were perforated with 9 mm, .40-caliber and 7.62 mm holes. Brognola jammed the transmission into Park and scooted back across the seat, booting open the passenger door. He pulled the mike off the dash and switched to the loudspeaker option on the Tac suite in the car. Dragging and snagging the mike with him, he crept out around the door using the hood and engine block as cover.

He keyed the mike.

"Groom Lake Security Personnel! This is Harold Brognola with the United States Justice Department! Surrender immediately! This facility is being shut down by order of the President of the United States! I repeat, you are ordered to surrender immediately or face possible mortal injury, as well as assured prosecution to the fullest extent of the federal law!"

The speech didn't inspire anyone on the opposing team to throw down weapons and wave a white flag. The responding gunfire seemed to increase.

Brognola dropped the mike and said over the tac net, "All units, this is Justice One. You are authorized to use whatever force is necessary to neutralize this resistance."

The scanner on the Tac suite squawked with incoming traffic. The scanner was set to the Stony Man internal frequency. Mack Bolan's voice was digitally reassembled from crypto and played back with a thousandth of a second delay.

"Justice One, is that you knocking at the back door?"

Brognola stayed low and retrieved the mike.

"Roger, Striker. Just extrapolating on satellite data from the Bear like you did. Figured you'd end up here."

"You have a great sense of timing."

"What's your twenty?"

"I'm rolling up to their rear in borrowed wheels."

"Are you experiencing heat?"

"Not anymore. Wait one. I'm making a play."

The line went dead and sixty seconds passed. Ninety. One-twenty.

Brognola retrieved the shotgun out of its cradle under the dash. He racked a round into the chamber and took aim over the hood of the car.

The flank of the Caprice absorbed more hailing abuse and rocked on the shocks with the impacts. More glass exploded, vomiting across the interior of the vehicle.

Brognola responded with a double buckshot volley aimed at the muzzle-flashes across the way when the glass had been blown across the interior of the car.

Outside Building 23

THE RADIO BARKED out traffic from the front.

"Trespassers have been stopped at intersection three-by-five. Send somebody around to flank them, over!"

Sector Agent in Charge Brad Kildare heard the vehicle screech to a halt directly behind him. He was standing behind the open door of his Jeep with an M-16 rifle pointed across the roof. Kildare craned around to look over his shoulder.

He gulped.

It was one of the men in black, the biggest, meanest-looking one he'd seen yet.

The guy was inches above six feet tall, stepping out of the passenger side of the Jeep and coming around the door, broad shouldered and dense with muscle. His black hair was matted with sweat and blood. The lines and angles of his grim face were streaked with cordite and other men's deaths. His blue eyes were ice fires of pure deep freeze.

He was wearing a black button-down dress shirt, black tie, black slacks and special black leather Oxford shoes. This guy wasn't wearing the suit coat as part of his ensemble. A black tactical assault vest was buckled across his chest, heavy with magazine cases, and over that was a special shoulder rig that tucked a weapon under each arm. Cradled in his hands was a big assault rifle Kildare almost mistook for a Heckler & Koch Model 91. But the barrel was too big around. He spied the tops of extra magazines peeking out from under tac nylon lids.

Those magazines were loaded with shotgun rounds.

A lithe guy with curly short hair wearing a flight suit got out of the driver's side. The flyboy covered Kildare with an Ingram MAC-10.

The MIB yelled at him, "Well, aren't you going to flank somebody around, asshole?"

Kildare jerked to attention and yelled back, "Yes, sir!"

He was conditioned to do anything an MIB told him without question. The security company had exdxtensive ties with the black projects of SENSOPS, and all their security personnel were screened for suitability in the "program." Once given a rubber-stamped seal of approval from the psychological-evaluation staff, the prospective security guard was sent for all-expenses-paid training in Las Vegas, run by SENSOPS. The training amounted to a mild brain-washing-behavior modification.

Kildare began to bellow into the mike clipped to his uniform epaulet. "All units north of four-by-six, flank south and reinforce the front in contact! Try to divide the enemy's fire! How copy, over?"

The units located to Kildare's immediate left rogered in. Four station identifications acknowledged receipt of the new instructions.

The security guards driving those four Jeeps jumped back into their vehicles, grinding transmissions in their haste to be first, and peeled out while trying to cut the others off.

"Great team spirit you engender here. Are you in charge of this mess?"

Kildare looked proud to admit it. "I am the sector agent. This is my sector."

"Well, all right, Sector Chief! This is what you need to do. You need to send half your guys out to the airfield."

Kildare looked suddenly confused. "Why? The airfield?"

The order had flattened his conditioning to automatically obey.

"Because there are enemy troops out there! I know—I've just been shooting it out with the bastards myself. You gonna keep asking dumb questions or are you going to cover our rear?"

"I'm going to cover the rear, sir!"

"Then do it!"

"Roger that, sir!"

Q Clearance Boulevard

"JUSTICE ONE, this is Striker, over."

Brognola snatched the mike off the seat next to him. "Go ahead."

"Heads up. You've got a flanking element that's going to hit you on the northeast side."

"I'll adjust accordingly. Thanks. Where are you now?"

"Making a little stopover. I believe I've found the local branch office of the same Nazi rat's nest I've been shutting down tonight. I'm going to recon by fire. See what runs for cover."

"I'll link up with you there."

"I'm cutting down on your workload. I just sent half their defense force out to the airfield to defend against a voodoo army."

"How do you do that?" Brognola asked.

"I play the alpha-male role pretty convincingly."

"That's your textbook answer."

"It's an ancient Polish secret. How's that for an answer?"

"Vague and cryptic."

"Gotta go. Don't forget your flank."

"Covered. Stay frosty."

Building 23, the Parking Garage

BOLAN AND GRIMALDI RAN down the up ramp and into the parking grotto. It was roomy down there, with a ceiling height of twelve, thirteen feet. The parking garage was easily three or four times the length and width of the admin building at ground level. The security company's fleet wasn't the only inventory warehoused here. There were tour buses refitted as government emergency command posts, earthmoving equipment, satellite broadcast vans, tractor trailers and Bradley APCs.

The elevator was located between the entry and exit ramps, and a card reader was the only way to hail a ride. Bolan pulled his FEMA Donato ID out of his pocket and ran the magnetic strip through the reader as the instruction diagram indicated.

The red light stayed on for what seemed an uncomfortable amount of time.

Finally, the light switched over to green and the elevator door opened.

Bolan frowned with satisfaction. His credit was still good here.

EXTENSION 23 WAS the agent tasked with being the gatekeeper for FEMA "management" inside Dreamland. The parking and vehicle storage levels extended three below the first. One elevator shaft connected them all with the single room on the ground floor of the admin building above.

The office of Extension 23.

To gain entrance to the inner sanctum, a person had to satisfy Extension 23, and he had some serious reach.

He was putting the finishing touches on the autodestruct sequence, and the two-minute silence count-down was initiated.

Nobody down below, even in the reactor core, suspected that the nuke was about to go off. At the mid-level of the secret underground compound that went two thousand feet below the earth was a thousand-megaton warhead buried in a concrete foundation pour. The doomsday button was wired to one desktop: Extension 23's.

He stood behind his desk on the raised platform that faced the elevator from the garage levels. He wore black SENSOPS-issued shades inside the overly bright room. He eyed the readouts on his desk. The elevator car had arrived.

The doors opened.

Extension 23 clapped his hands and recognized the great human spirit that stepped into the sterile white octagonal room.

He said, "Welcome, Mr. Donato. Or is it, Mr. *Bolan*. Newport got a warning off before he bit the bygone."

The big SENSOPS impostor grinned. "Call me whatever you want. It's your funeral."

"Then it is our funeral together, Bolan. Before you blast away, come check out my desk readouts here."

He looked at Grimaldi. "You too, bat boy. We don't have time for the stare down."

The two Stony Man warriors mounted the short stairs up to the man's desk. Bolan's eyes narrowed as he came around the desk and scanned the readout.

"What's about to blow?"

The Executioner jammed the muzzle of the auto-shotgun into Extension 23's face as incentive.

"A strategic nuclear warhead."

He was satisfied to see the color drain from Bolan's face.

"Strategic? What size?"

"Ten megs, big boy." The MIB didn't seem at all concerned about the fact that he was going to be vaporized along with everything else on the base.

Bolan swore. "How deep?"

"Eight Hundred."

Bolan looked at the clock. 01:32, 01:31...

The Executioner said, "Touché," shouldering and firing the 12-gauge combat shotgun into the man's face from a range of about two feet.

Grimaldi jumped back to avoid the flying gore, and cursed.

"We've got to get the hell out of here, Jack, or we're toast."

There was only one door out of the strange checkpoint, and it was behind the desk. They both bolted.

THERE WERE NO EXITS in the building. The first floor was nothing but mortar and bulletproof glass. The only way out, apparently, was back through the parking garages. But there was no time for that.

"Jesus Christ, Sarge!" Grimaldi said. "What kind of a screwy building is this?"

"The wrong kind to be stuck in when a 1K nuke is about to go off."

Bolan shouldered through the first doorway on his

left. It was a copier-fax room with shelves of paper supplies. The fax was bleeping and in reception mode. The room had a big armored picture window, which Bolan had been counting on. He shouldered the autoshotgun and fired the remaining seven slugs into the center of the window, making a tight X. The bolt locked back, empty and hungry for more.

The Executioner thumbed the mag-release switch by letting go of the trigger and reaching forward while his left hand went to the correct ammo pouch. He plucked out the HE rounds and slid the magazine into the well, tapping the bottom of the mag twice to make sure it was seated and locked.

He shouldered the weapon as he hit the bolt release. The bolt jerked forward and rammed the first bomb into the chamber. He memorized the sight picture, then stepped into the hall, closing the door enough to allow part of his arm and the shotgun through the crack.

Grimaldi was already down low and braced against the opposite wall in the hall.

"Fire in the hole," Bolan said and fired the little jewel.

The HE package was an impact-detonation device with a warhead that amounted to a few teaspoons of crystalline plastique. It was a perfect antipersonnel explosive round, guaranteed to blow men to bleeding chunks up to one hundred yards out.

The explosion was terrific and blew Bolan out of the doorway, tossing him like a rag doll across the hall. He got to his feet, then booted what was left of the door off the hinges and went into the wrecked, smoking room. The place was hazy with acrid smoke from seared plastic, and he held his breath. The window and frame were mostly gone. Getting out of the building was no longer an obstacle. The Executioner jumped through and Grimaldi was right behind him.

Bolan alerted the Feds while sprinting for the Jeep.

"Justice One, bail out! Bail out now! Turn and run for the fence line! There's a nuke about to go off right under us!"

HAL BROGNOLA KNEW Bolan wasn't one for crying wolf.

But that one word was all that was needed to paint one bloody ugly picture. *Nuke.* This part of Nevada was probably the most nuked place in the world. He didn't want to become part of the history of underground testing.

Brognola jumped behind the wheel of the powerful Caprice, tossing the riot shotgun into the back seat. The engine was still running, and he didn't bother with the door. He shifted into reverse and stomped the gas.

He was barking a steady stream of orders over the radio as he came about.

"All units, turn and run for the fence line! A nuclear device about to detonate is underground this base!"

Brognola hit the brakes and spun the wheel. The heavy car's nose swapped places with its trunk in a mist of fine dust. He shifted into Drive as the car door slammed hard. He put the gas pedal to the floor and boomed back for the open desert via Q Clearance Boulevard.

There was about a half mile of nothing to the gate.

"SWAT One commander, get your men on the road and start running until I get to you! I'll throw open some doors and you can jump in!"

SWAT One came back with the new sitrep.

"We have a civilian female here and prisoners. Over."

"All units, how copy SWAT One's situation? I need some of you people out there to follow me through the gates. We've got to get everybody out. Nobody's left behind."

Brognola didn't have to worry about support. It looked like his troops were following him out, confident that, like Moses, he could lead them to the safety on the other side.

He just hoped that they had enough time to make it back to the gates.

BOLAN PAUSED long enough to tell the sector chief what the score was.

"You might want to haul ass for the fence line, you and your boys. Your boss is cooking off a real big nuke right underneath us."

Grimaldi was already behind the wheel and turning over the engine.

"Sarge!"

Bolan leaped into the car as Grimaldi dropped into Drive and screeched around the sector chief's vehicle.

The soldier held on to the dash and let the sharp turn left, then right, slam his door for him. Grimaldi was bombing for an edge of the base pointing close to south. He was going to race straight across the alkali flats until he sliced through that chain link like a runaway locomotive. And if they made it that far, hopefully, it would be far enough.

The Executioner's combat biocomputer was ticking off the numbers, comparing that decay rate with the distance they had to go.

Something was going to have to be bent between here and there.

Numbers didn't lie.

THE PILOT OF Airborne Two transmitted to the net, "Roger. Airborne One and Three are evacuating. I'm hanging back to look for your guy, Justice One."

Brognola came back with, "Yank them out if it looks like they're not going to make it."

"I'm prepared to break the laws of physics, Justice One."

"You break the laws of Jesus, God, and Mary if that's what it takes to get those men out alive. Understand?"

"If I fail, should I crash the helicopter?"

"What?"

"Sorry, Justice One, just a little poop there to go with the mound of shit you're already buried in."

IT WAS CHAFING Grimaldi fiercely not knowing.

The Jeep was clear of the base and racing across

the flats toward the fence line at close to eighty. The
SUV was bouncing like a rude fun-park ride. Bolan
stared straight ahead, cold and silent. Grimaldi knew
that the guy was counting it down himself.

"So, how long we got?"

Bolan didn't look over at his longtime friend.

"About nineteen seconds."

"Oh. It's been nice knowing you."

"It's not over till it's over, right?"

"Always the diehard optimist, aren't you?"

BROGNOLA ROARED UP on the South Gate, slowing
on approach. There was a line of a dozen Caprices,
Crown Victorias and vans playing train right behind
him. On the flanks to each side of Q Clearance Boulevard were the rest of the task force vehicles, running
in a straight-line front for the hunter-orange fence
line.

Seeing that his precious cargo wasn't standing in
the containment area with thumbs up looking for a
ride, Brognola bombed right through and spotted
them about one hundred yards south up the improved
road that took over from the pavement of Q
Clearance.

Brognola went to the airwaves with his hasty concept of this operation. "Next two units right in line
behind me, take it to the shoulder when I do. The rest
of you just keep going. We're getting the hell out of
your way. Don't stop until you're either singing with
the choir in Heaven or you know for sure that you've

beaten the house odds by seeing the lights of Vegas. Good luck, everybody.''

Brognola took it to the shoulder.

BOLAN HAD ON the NVGs he'd found stashed in the console between the front seats. He could see the fence line clearly in the light-amplified distance. Still about a thousand yards to go. So close and yet so far.

"I'm out of numbers!" Grimaldi yelled.

"Not quite yet," Bolan said calmly.

Grimaldi's heart thudded twice.

"Now we are out of numbers," Bolan announced grimly.

THE GROUND EFFECTS of the detonation were indistinguishable from a major earthquake. The nuclear device served only one purpose: to conceal the truth. The bomb was their fail-safe. Extension 23 was more than a gatekeeper. He was an insurance claims adjuster, as well. If compromise of the Area 51 operation seemed imminent, Extension 23 was the insurance that the dirty laundry got lost, forever in a nuclear slag heap with a half-life of at least a century.

Everything aboveground at Groom Lake was window dressing for what was below, out of sight. The *real* Area 51 couldn't be seen from Freedom Ridge. Area 51 was the complex under Groom Lake.

Was.

Everything beneath Building 23 was being vaporized from the bottom up in a miniature solar fireball that would burn anything.

The pressure of the blast forced everything up; the surface bubbled like a giant mile-wide dome. Building 23 marked the center of the effect; the elevator shaft that connected all levels of the secret complex to the surface made for an excellent exhaust vent. It was the reverse of Sodom and Gomorrah. The column of fire came from under the earth, not Heaven, and Building 23 was reduced to ash in the twinkling of an eye. The serpentine lick of atomic fire was a whole city block around and coiled three hundred feet into the sunless night. At its apex, the column lost cohesion and fell apart, raining superheated radioactive brimstone onto the roofs of the surface buildings of the Groom Lake base. Like dry kindling, the base went up in flames.

Those caught inside that fiendish perimeter didn't make it.

With the upward pressure vented, the dome reversed and the sickening cave-in to man-made Hell began.

THE GROUND WAVE HIT the Jeep from the rear and sent the speeding SUV nose forward on a flip. The roof traded places with the tires, the windshield collapsed and a fantail of dirt and rock sprayed over the two men as the vehicle carved a shallow grave in the caliche soil.

The sport utility rocked back and lifted the hood out of the dirt. Bolan, upside down with the NVGs still in place, saw the land rolling away toward the south, like a ripple running through a flicked towel.

At the same time, the slope of the ground was increasing. The desert was puffing up its chest. In greenish misty digital detail, Bolan saw the fence line rise in the ground swell and all the real estate for at least a quarter mile beyond.

Everything that rose had to come down.

Bolan knew what was coming next—the rollback and cave-in.

At least fifteen hundred yards had to be traveled before the earth beneath the two soldiers' feet would fall away into an atomic blast furnace. Bolan knew all about the limits to flesh and bone mechanics. Trying to run that far while the earth was convulsing was a feat for comic-book superheroes.

He knew that it was impossible to even try.

But what was impossible for Bolan to visualize was staying where he was and waiting for the end. Doing nothing. Just giving up. No more struggle. No more fight.

Bolan released the shoulder safety harness and held on, twisting out from under the dash and dropping to his haunches on the roof that was now the floor. Grimaldi did likewise. Most of the glass on the vehicle was gone. They had no problem exiting. Bolan didn't bother with trying to retrieve the SWA-12. That would burn precious seconds and in this foot race, every second was irretrievable.

Bolan and Grimaldi came out from under each side of the Jeep, negotiating the tight quarters like an Army obstacle on a timed course. Both of them got to their feet at the same time and ran. The ground didn't stay in one place and was spongy underneath the balls of their feet. Like running in deep sand.

The Executioner knew immediately that they weren't going to make it.

He threw away the NVGs and ran harder.

The rumble behind the Stony Man warriors was increasing in volume. Grinding, snapping, popping and tumbling away—simultaneous events in combination, each with a distinct doom-sealing sound.

Bolan didn't look back; it would just slow his stride.

He wasn't going to look back and he wasn't going to stop. He'd keep moving as long as he had a body to move with. Death would take him fighting. No quarters given. And none asked for. Just make it a good fight. It was the best a man could do.

The buckling earth overtook them, and the ground dropped suddenly beneath their feet.

This was it.

Bolan and Grimaldi touched down after a ten-foot drop; the desert floor had sheared away and plummeted. They were driven to their knees by the impact. A wall of loose dirt and rock described the geology of what had just happened. Both of them were up in an instant and running to attack the steep slope that would get them back up to ground level again.

They scrambled up the incline, desperate to clear the top.

The world was dissolving in seismic mayhem; the shear line could give way for the final plunge any second. The dirt face of the exposed fault was mimicking water and moving in a current. The low-in-the-bones bass note was everywhere, agitating earth and air.

Bolan and Grimaldi crabbed over the lip and crawled to get some distance from that edge. The two of them started to stand.

Then all at once the roof caved in, the Groom Lake facility was gone and the ground underneath their feet was about to join in the collapse. Bolan and Grimaldi sprinted for the fence line. Whole football-field-sized chunks of the orange chain link were down, bowled over by the ground wave.

Grimaldi was panting like a dog.

"Sarge, man. I mean it now. It's been a hell of a life and a hell of an honor serving with you."

"We've got to make it to the fence line, Jack," Bolan said.

Grimaldi was going to respond but something absolutely unexpected happened. It robbed him of words. The hellish din of the cave-in was partially masked by the air-smacking throb and telltale whirlwind of a helicopter buzzing the ground at fifteen feet. The chopper went over their heads and dropped a dozen yards in front of them, hovering, skimming the trembling soil. The two door snipers were leaning out both sides of the aircraft on tethers, yelling at them, waving them in on the final stretch to home plate.

Each of them took a side of the helicopter and hopped up on the skid. They grabbed on to outstretched arms, and outstretched arms grabbed on to them. The JetRanger went into a full-throttle power climb to the south, gaining distance and altitude at a stomach-churning rate. As Bolan was yanked inside, he glanced down and saw the ground below disintegrate and crumble away.

The Executioner was delivered.

And then, in an instant, the miracle went sour and the engines, radios, everything mechanical being run by electronic circuitry of any kind overloaded and blew out.

BROGNOLA WAS STILL a little dazed, trying to figure out what precisely had hit them. It came from the rear, went under the car and continued like a rocket across the landscape. The front end of the Caprice was buried in a crack in the road. The engine was dead. Brognola tried to turn over the ignition and fire the sparks. Nothing. The radio was dead. Scattered to his right and left across the flats were the vehicles of the task force. At least half of the cars and vans were on their sides or tires up, wheels spitting dirt into the air. The men in vehicles that hadn't flipped over were EVA, helping the ones who had been sent doing cartwheels in their cars by the seismic shock front of the huge underground detonation.

He happened to look at his watch and realized that the second hand wasn't moving anymore. He shook his wrist and put the watch to his ear. Still nothing. The watch was electronic like everything else on the planet at the dawn of the twenty-first century.

And then it hit him: the EM pulse.

On the heels of that thought came the follow-on, and Brognola's stomach did a butterfly free fall.

The helicopters. All three of them were down now, as sure as shit. That had to be the first priority here. Find the downed choppers and get the survivors out. He didn't even know if Airborne Two had pulled Striker and Jack out in time.

It was the not knowing that propelled him out of the dead car like a jaguar on adrenaline. He pulled a bullhorn with him and triggered it, but his voice wasn't being amplified.

"Goddammit!"

He threw the useless bullhorn back into the car and ran toward the largest group of marshals, yelling instructions.

"I need three teams. Those choppers are down somewhere around us. Everything is down due to the EM pulse from that blast. I want each team to have a 203 with illumination rounds for signaling. When you find a chopper, put illumination into the air to mark your location. Let's move it!"

MACK BOLAN HAD no idea how long he'd been out cold. He woke up facedown in the dirt. Somebody yelling "Over here!" brought him back to the scene, and he groaned as the pain from multiple contusions and abrasions went screaming through his brain on the heels of regaining consciousness. He rolled over and sat up, gratified that everything seemed to bend and flex normally. There was no grinding of broken bones or torn ligaments.

The Executioner looked around to get his bearings. The smoking wreckage of the JetRanger was located about fifty yards uprange of his position. From the looks of the desert floor between Bolan and the crashed helicopter, the chopper had skipped like a stone upon making contact with the ground, and one of those skips had ejected Bolan right out the open door. A group of federal marshals was running toward him, and he recognized Hal Brognola leading the charge.

Bolan stood and dusted himself off.

"Well," Bolan said, "I'm glad you decided to stay out of the office this week, Hal."

"Are you all right?"

The soldier shrugged. "No worse for the wear. What about everybody else? What about Jack?"

"No casualties yet, but I don't know about the crew of the other two helicopters. Two other search parties are still trying to find them. Jack's okay. He broke his pinkie in the crash."

"Ouch."

"The EM pulse has completely knocked out everything. We have no commo and no wheels. It's going to be a long walk back to Vegas."

"Oh, I think we should just sit tight. That blast didn't go unnoticed, Hal. This place is going to be crawling with every alphabet-soup agency soon trying to figure out who set off a nuke. Trust me, we'll have a ride out of here soon."

Brognola looked toward the Groom Lake facility. What was left after the cave-in was still burning weirdly, lighting the predawn sky with brush strokes of pink, orange and red.

"It would probably be a good idea to start walking, don't you think? What about fallout?"

"The fallout will be negligible. The cave-in will contain most of it, and the wind is blowing toward the north. We should be safe."

Brognola grunted. "Should be, sure. Famous last words."

To the south, a muffled pop carried on the breeze turned the two men's heads in that direction. Something pyrotechnic was lofting into the sky on a trail of sparks, then a parachute flare came to life in the clear sky like a miniature sun radiating pink light.

"Looks like somebody found one of the other choppers," Brognola commented.

"You ready?"

"Yeah."

"Then let's go."

EPILOGUE

FEMA was activated in the region by the people now left running the agency who believed just as the American public did: FEMA was in the business of disaster relief. And that's what the American public was being fed on all major networks. The incident in Nevada, near Groom Lake, was an earthquake along a fault line created in the fifties by nuclear testing. High-pressure water being injected into local wells had lubed the fault, causing it to shift suddenly.

In cyberspace, the cover-up wasn't washing at all. It all revolved around the hysterical post dated November 22 at 17:31 Nevada local time on the newsgroup alt.area51.government.cover.up by the cybercitizen branding himself "The_Bern69." The_Bern69 wrote:

"I just got back from Freedom Ridge. I was there. I've got video to prove what I saw. The TV and government are lying. What happened out there wasn't an earthquake. I think my hair is falling out, and earthquakes don't make hair fall out. Federal agents were in the process of

raiding Area 51 when a nuke was detonated under the base. There was fire, fallout. It was like
seeing Armageddon in real life.

The post then vectored straight into the twilight
zone.

The government nuked the grays living under
Area 51 to prevent any more gray-manufactured
clones of our leaders from entering public service manipulating policy to actualize an alien
agenda. I used to have a source inside A-51 that
assured me this was what was really going on at
the base. The grays want this planet for coloni-
zation but they have to exterminate us first.''

The_Bern69 was one of those UFOers who fer-
vently believed that the ''grays'' were really a bunch
of reptile-insectoid space Nazis from Zeta Reticuli.
The_Bern69's account contained a postscript about
video footage shot from Freedom Ridge on the same
night by Beth Fletcher.

A former colleague of mine was on Freedom
Ridge that night but she bailed out before the
real show began. Sure, she has some neat footage. But mine is better! Beth Fletcher is an op-
portunist who will say anything to garner the
limelight for herself. Take any claims she makes
about me or my tape with a grain of salt.

He ended the post with several stills taken from the video itself. The pictures were provocative. Hired experts for the government said that the stills were "neat special effects."

The Nevada "earthquake" monopolized attention, and little was ever heard about the massacre in west Texas. That news stayed local. And life went on.

A rat pack had been stomped, and the ripples of that event had shifted outcomes.

The republic still had a few more sunrises left.

James Axler

OUTLANDERS®

TIGERS OF HEAVEN

In the Outlands, the struggle for control of the baronies continues. Kane, Grant and Brigid seek allies in the Western Islands empire of New Edo, where they try to enlist the aid of the Tigers of Heaven, a group of samurai warriors.

Book #2 of the Imperator Wars saga, a trilogy chronicling the introduction of a new child imperator—launching the baronies into war!

**A journey through the dangerous frontier
known as the future...**

JAMES AXLER
DEATH LANDS®

Zero City

Hungry and exhausted, Ryan and his band emerge from
a redoubt into an untouched predark city, and uncover a
cache of weapons and food. Among other interlopers,
huge winged creatures guard the city. Holed up inside
an old government building, where Ryan's son, Dean,
lies near death, Ryan and Krysty must raid where a local
baron uses human flesh as fertilizer....

Take 2 explosive books plus a mystery bonus
FREE

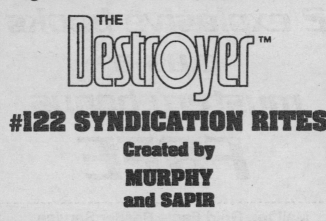